...are spent with
... and Mr Tiggs, a feline with
...w that one day I would write romantic
...but I never dreamed they would have a psychic twist!
...ve experienced many 'unexplainable' things, but it took a
...ng time for me to accept the reality of what that means.
...ve, life and beyond…but it's ALWAYS about the romance!

Forbidden

LINN B. HALTON

HarperImpulse an imprint of
HarperCollins*Publishers* Ltd
77–85 Fulham Palace Road
Hammersmith, London W6 8JB

www.harpercollins.co.uk

A Paperback Original 2014

First published in Great Britain in ebook format by HarperImpulse 2013

Cover Images © Shutterstock.com

Linn B. Halton asserts the moral right to
be identified as the author of this work

A catalogue record for this book is
available from the British Library

ISBN: 9780007591633

This novel is entirely a work of fiction.
The names, characters and incidents portrayed in it are
the work of the author's imagination. Any resemblance to
actual persons, living or dead, events or localities is
entirely coincidental.

Automatically produced by Atomik ePublisher from Easypress

I would like to thank Kim, Heidi, Kate, JB, Erin, Susan, Shaz, Charlotte, Dizzy C, Nikki and Tobi for valued feedback and support - love you guys! Also Mandy for being a listening ear and for her constant support and guidance.

To my friends and colleagues at Loveahappyending Lifestyle emagazine - writers who share their knowledge and from whom I've learnt so much!

To all of the HarperImpulse team - for your energy, enthusiasm and the buzz you create that writers and readers are loving so much!

Lastly I have to thank 'my rock', Lawrence, without you by my side I wouldn't be able to devote all of my time to writing...

CERI

Prologue

The Ethereal Pathway

I'm in a tunnel. It's dark and yet little rays, like pinpricks of sunshine breaking through foliage, seep towards me from every angle. Too minute to light my path, I wonder if they are really threads drawing me along in case I lose my way. My body is cold and I feel disconnected, as if I'm no longer whole. Alex is calling my name, his voice distant. I want to find my way back to him but I'm being coaxed away, carried on a wave of light within a dark place. Am I dreaming? Will this moment pass and then I'll simply wake up next to Alex, content in the knowledge that the future stretches out ahead of us?

Fear takes control of my mind. I want to go back. I'm frightened and I don't want to be in this place. It seems I am incapable of doing anything and the fact that I don't have a choice is terrifying.

Ceri's journey continues...

Chapter One – Transition

Something instinctive tells me that I have to make some sense of this quickly. The memory I have of the past is draining away, like sand running through a sieve into a black hole. Fragments of thoughts that are clear one moment, then hazy before my mind can play each one through to a conclusion. Is someone trying to erase my past, one memory at a time? Why have I been pulled into this vortex where time doesn't seem to be relative to anything?

I try to concentrate. What's the last thing I can remember? The sunshine was streaming in through the window and I turned over to find Alex lying next to me. My world felt complete and I was happier than I had been in a long while. I knew beyond a shadow of a doubt that Alex would love me forever, no matter what the future held. Someone told me I was an angel, but I can only recall the voice and not the face of the person speaking to me. Was it Alex? There was a warning… yes! The voice told me that Alex and I were not destined to be together and we had broken one of the cardinal rules: angels don't fall in love with their spirit helpers.

I feel as if I'm being pulled in two directions at the same time. Which way should I turn? I realise that I'm no longer attached to my earthly shell. The next part of my journey has begun.

My heart cries out for Alex, for his love. I won't let go, I won't let go…

Chapter Two – The Healing

As my confusion lifts it's like peeling back layers of old paint. Each layer reveals something new and the deeper I delve, the closer I'm getting to the truth. I never believed Ethan Morris's words when he put forward his theory that I was an angel. Wouldn't I *know* if that were the case? Now I'm here – wherever it is – I'm not so sure, because this is such a weird experience. Have I died? Or maybe I'm in a coma. All I know for sure is I've never experienced anything like this before.

There is a strange feeling of familiarity I can't explain, though, a sense of knowing this place. I'm no longer scared, merely waiting for what comes next. I don't think this is the first time I've been in this situation. Have I come home to the place where I truly belong?

It isn't an unpleasant feeling, this sense of disconnection. It's rather restful. Time and space don't seem relevant anymore but I feel protected, as if someone is watching over me and guiding me along. Maybe I've been in an accident and I'm unconscious. That might be the reason why I can't feel anything in relation to my body. I try to reach out with my thoughts, hoping someone is listening and will engage with me. I can't seem to…

It hits me as hard as running into a brick wall. My head is suddenly full of a million thoughts. Memories whizz through my mind so fast and yet each one is familiar and meaningful.

Ethan was right.

I want to cry out in anguish as Alex's face appears before me. I find myself trying to reach out into the darkness, then realise none of this is physical. I'm in a void where there is nothing except my thoughts and memories. This is where our spirit returns when we are in transition: that place of nothingness where we rest.

All mental blocks are lifted. I remember that as an angel sent to administer on the earth plane, my vibration is restricted for a reason. All knowledge falls away and only a sense of knowing allows me to fulfil my allotted tasks. I remember little on my return here each night, when my earthly energy is in deep sleep, because that is the rule. My place and purpose in the universe is all-consuming. I now understand that a small part of me is bound to the earth until that part of my destiny is played out. It is only here that I can see the true nature of everything.

Then there is a presence. It's one I know and love dearly: someone who has been with me since my earliest memory. Each energy has its own unique identity, like an aura, but crossing the divide between the planes changes things. Here, everything is constant and our minds link with ease.

"You have a purity that means you are special. Few angels are chosen to touch the earth and carry out their work on that plane. We trust in you to rise above the burdens that weigh down souls in their mortal life. We know there are no guarantees and so many things can go wrong. All you can do is to be receptive and hold on to the knowledge that you are different."

"But what if I fail?" I ask, fearful of the unknown. Of all of the tasks I have been given, this seems the hardest. I'd heard so many tales about the coldness of human life, of the hardship and stark reality… which I now understood with heart-breaking consequences. I knew there was beauty too, of course, even before I set foot there. Few angels ever talked about an earthly life, our vibration being on a different level to those energies who work tirelessly there.

There is so much more to the state of being than touching earth, no matter how many times some souls make the journey. Here, we gravitate towards like-minded energies. The level at which we work is irrelevant as there is no status, only purpose. I've enjoyed so many sectors of being: the nearer I draw to the core, the more I become a part of the whole and a little more of 'me' is lost. I wonder if I am destined for the highest honour, whether I am a splinter of the Source.

Of course, no one knows for sure that splinters really exist. Wider knowledge can only be given when it's appropriate. I believe that splinters will only gain that understanding when there is a call-back: a time when the Source of all being chooses to reunite all of the elements to its core. That would effect a critical change upon the universe, which I'm led to believe has only happened a few times. The Source of us all is benevolent.

On some planes, like earth, the decision was made that energy has to learn from making bad choices as well as good. Core change ripples outwards and whilst it will bring great joy to some, to others it will bring misery. Humans have affected the planet around which their lives revolve and there are serious consequences. It has upset the balance of things and it seems to be a pattern that is repeated, like a never ending circle. The only way to ensure earth continues is for change to be implemented at the highest level, to help redress the imbalance.

The next core change will be to bring back something that has been lost: closeness to the inner-self and the intuitive nature within all humans. On the ethereal plane we have all sensed this with growing concern. I feel I am destined to be a part of implementing that wider change. How exactly, I have no idea. There are times when I know things I can't possibly have learnt, things that come naturally to me.

I struggle to recall my memories, but transitioning back to my higher level energy now is draining and I have to be patient. It's a time of healing and when I'm recovered all will be revealed to me. A human's face appears in my consciousness for one brief moment and I feel a sharp stab of pain.

Do I know this man?

***

Healing is a time of rest, a time to wander with no agenda and I'm not totally comfortable with the sense of freedom and disconnection. It's often interesting, of course, merely watching other energies and souls as they go about their work. It too can be a beneficial part of the learning process, but I worry as there is still so much work to be done.

On my vibration level there are many I do not know and it's always a blessing to find myself travelling through space filled with new and interesting energies. There is so much to learn! But the best experience of all is when I'm with my own group. Energies that have been around me since time began. Souls with whom I will ways be linked forever, because in essence we are the same: we are family. Where our future journey will take us, I do not know, only that we will be together. Are we splinters? Will our energy levels become fulfilled to the point where we will have the power to change things? A time when the supreme energy, the centre of the cosmos, will call upon us to help renew the force that holds all the ethereal and life planes together? Are we perpetuity? I seriously doubt that splinters can simply acquire the knowledge. Some of it has to be learnt and developed, because that's how it works. The group might then come together to harness that power under direction. The idea both excites and frightens me.

Then I remember that I have now touched earth, a part of me is still there and the fact that I'm back in transition means something has gone wrong. I wish I could remember and can only assume that after my time in healing it will become clear.

I only know that I'm experiencing something new. I've never had a sensation quite like this, as if a part of me is missing. How can that be? Our essence and energy is one complete mass. Before my trip I didn't know any different, but now I have this sensation of having left something behind. How strange, or is that how it's supposed to be? I'm being impatient and I try to let the healing do its work. How I've missed the tranquillity of the universe; there is an incredibly harsh edge to life on the earth plane that grates on the soul. Such conflict – beauty and horror; happiness and sadness; love and hate. I wonder how the working energies cope with their many visits, and whether each of their mortal lives is different. With every mission being to help a soul on their life path, do they too return and feel a little part of their own energy has been left behind?

Healing claims me and I revel in the purity of feeling renewed. It blocks out everything else and a sense of peace begins to gather around me.

Chapter Three – Trust

"Ceri?"

A voice floats into my mind, bringing me back into consciousness.

"You are still in transition. The part of you that remains on earth will restrict your consciousness. Your energy is split and will remain so until you are recalled permanently. I will always be with you, until you are fully back with us. The human element sometimes hampers our communication, but I'm by your side every step of the way."

I fleetingly remember the sensation of this presence, the energy who guides me. It is a feeling of wisdom and I have a desire to please him, to excel simply in order to bask in his approval.

"Have I done something wrong? It seems that way. I thought I'd forgotten, but now I remember. Is it to do with Alex?"

"Yes. We did not take the decision to let you touch the earth plane lightly. You are one of the splinters, and it is necessary for your development. You need to experience the emotions of the human plane if, when your time comes, your energy is going to be a part of renewing the force that controls everything. It isn't easy and things do go wrong. However, we are confused. Alex is the soul we have chosen to help you move onto the next part of your work on earth. You are destined to channel messages. It is your role to help many on their earthly path towards an understanding of the true nature of spirituality. Without the comfort of those personal messages from their kindred energies here, they will be hampered. Human life is a constant struggle for all believers and this is a vital element linking the two planes."

"I see. He was helping me, I think. I remember wavering, unsure what to believe. Is that normal for an angel's earth life?"

"There is no norm, few angels visit earth. It isn't necessary for their work. In your case, your experience will be enough to inform the kindred group when the time comes. There is only a need to feel those emotions that are peculiar to the earth plane and pass on that experience for understanding. That's the whole point of human life: extremes. Love here is pure, as are our energies, but to truly understand the whole of creation it is necessary to experience how life develops. Every single thing that happens on the earth plane is very real to the beings experiencing it, although there is no lasting relevance as such. It is simply about learning. Alex is a lesser energy, very young, and a part of his fate is to provide sympathy and comfort while you adjust to your next step on earth. He is merely a spirit helper and will go on to complete his own destiny to allow his energy to grow. You cannot be together Ceri. He never will be on your vibration level. He is not a splinter."

I feel elated, saddened, and chastised all at the same time. I want to make amends and prove that this was merely an aberration, a period of adjustment when I didn't know what I was supposed to be doing. Will I be forgiven?

"There is no need for forgiveness Ceri," his words fill my head. "Simply follow the path laid out."

"What happens now?" I feel uncomfortable, unable to understand exactly how this works. A part of me wonders whether it will be as easy as following a path.

"Instead of only returning here when your earthly shell is in a resting state, we'll adjust the amount of your energy that stays on the earth plane. You will continue to carry out your duties here permanently, but simply be less productive. A part of you will continue to see out your earthly experience until that is due to come to an end."

"When will that be?"

"Another fifty-two earth years."

"How will this affect my earthly person? If I'm not there in full strength, will I still be able to fulfil what is required of me? Won't that hamper my ability to channel messages?" The concern I feel is unsettling.

"No, it will not lessen your psychic ability, as they refer to it on earth. But as you go about your work you will have an awareness of your ethereal existence. We regard this as a situation that isn't ideal. You might be tempted to share things that are not meant to be known earth-side. The two planes are very different. Human life is a training ground. No more, no less. But it is necessary and it has a purpose. So we're asking that you consider everything you do there from this point on with the benefit of your wider knowledge. Some of that will simply not make sense down there, Ceri, if you share it with a human." Hearing him use my earthly name is strange. It's out of place here.

"I'm not sure I'm strong enough…"

"No one can be sure of anything, until they try. We have ways of limiting damage, but this too is a part of your development. If you change things, then you will have to deal with the consequences. It's time for you to go back now."

As the voice floats out of my mind I remember Alex. Why didn't I ask the question?

How long will Alex be in my life and when will I have to let him go?

Chapter Four – Eyes Wide Open

"Hey, morning sleepy head." Alex adjusts the duvet, snuggling it around me as I bring myself back. I do a double-take as his head seems to shimmer, his aura clearly visible to me now with my heightened awareness. There is a sense of purity around him and I can't believe I couldn't see that before. How did I not recognise he was a helper, a young energy in training?

"Good," I try to sound calm.

Alex moves around the bedroom tidying things away before heading out the door. The energy radiating from his body resembles electric sparks.

"I'll make some coffee," he says over his shoulder as he disappears.

I pull myself up into a sitting position and slump back against the pillows. Oh my God! I really am still here, only it feels different.

The voice comes into my head. "Don't worry, you are adjusting and things will settle down. Give it time."

The silence in my head leaves a void which is quickly replaced by a stream of questions I can't seem to stem. How long will it take? Will Alex notice a difference in me? What should I say to him? I realise I'm in danger of hyperventilating, my hands grabbing onto the duvet and making two fists, the tension radiating up my arms. I lie back, taking a few slow, deep breaths. I close my eyes. Outside

I can hear the birds and the faint sound of traffic. Is this the same morning that I was called back to transition, or has time passed here on earth? How will I explain what has happened to Alex?

Suddenly I feel as if someone has placed an arm around my shoulders and there is a sensation of great warmth. I wonder if it's going to lift me physically from the bed, it's so intense, but the moment passes. I'm not alone and understanding that helps a little.

Alex returns, humming a tune under his breath. The moment he walks back into the room, two steaming mugs of coffee in his hands, his face breaks out into a radiant smile.

"The first day of the rest of our lives." He sounds so happy, and I realise that to him there has been no disruption. I send a prayer of thanks out into the ether to my mentor. I need all the help I can get.

I take the coffee mug from him and return his smile. I try my best to match his air of unfettered optimism. "You sound cheerful."

His fingers brush against mine as he releases the mug. He lingers a moment before drawing away.

"I feel like celebrating," he muses, as if his mind is churning and he hasn't yet had time to process what's happening. He sounds like a kid, really excited and it's a big deal – he's about to open his Christmas presents or something. There's a liveliness about him and he can't seem to sit still. He walks to the window and looks out into the street.

"I wish I didn't have to go to work today," he mutters, more to himself than to me. "You know, I think last night was the first time I didn't have a bad dream. About us, I mean."

I'm fascinated by the glow that emanates around his upper body, pulsating gently, softening his outline. The clarity is breathtaking: Alex might not be an angel, but he's an energy that exudes healing and positivity. I long to get up and throw my arms around him, but I'm not sure my legs would carry me that few feet between the bed and the window. Even lying here, propped up against the pillows, I feel shaky and unsteady. I sip my coffee, hoping the caffeine will do the trick and begin to ground my thoughts.

"You stirred earlier and began talking to me, but you were still dreaming," he turns to face me, a little furrow on his brow. "Can you remember your dream? You thought something was wrong. I shushed you and you fell back to sleep. You aren't having dreams about us, are you?" he asks, tentatively, trying to hide his concern.

"No, I don't think so. I'm fine now, although I think I might be coming down with a sore throat," I offer, wanting… no, *needing* to reassure him and stop him dwelling on what happened.

"Good. You would tell me if you thought something was wrong, wouldn't you? You don't regret our decision to be together?"

His words are like a bolt of lightning. Now that I am consciously aware of the position we're in, and with an insight into both existences, how can I answer that question?

"Of course not." Fortunately my tone is even. I take a large gulp of my coffee to give me a few moments more to adjust.

Alex saunters over to sit down next to me on the bed.

"I want to explain." His eyes search my face, lovingly, like a gentle kiss. "I only sought out Ethan Morris because I was worried about what my dreams seemed to be telling me. After you asked me to leave I realised that I hadn't meant any of the words I had thrown at you. I was panicking because I couldn't figure out why loving you felt so wrong, so selfish. As if I wasn't putting your interests first, only thinking about what I wanted. When you disappeared I was frantic. All I could think about was whether you were safe and it hurt knowing that my outburst was a knee-jerk reaction to my fear. I know this must all sound a bit weird, Ceri, but I've loved you for so long. Since the first day we began working together. It was a long two years, being next to you five days a week and carrying this burden, this feeling that I must not let you know how madly in love I am with you. You kept it professional and I took that to mean you didn't feel the same way in return. I now understand that it's hard for you to show anyone the side of you that is different. It's a gift that makes living your life very hard at times. When you opened up to me and we ended up in bed, I was so happy and so scared. I'm sorry Ceri, you were right, we make our own future. You have a gift and maybe that was freaking me out a little. Ethan believes what he preaches, but who's to know how it all works? After all, we have free will – it says so in the Bible."

His words take me by surprise. I realise that when I ran away it must have been a real shock to Alex. I didn't want to believe what he'd told me about Ethan's theory either, but all of his concerns seem to have disappeared overnight. Has something changed in Alex that I can't see? His level of vibration is much lower than an angel's and he's not supposed to have conscious knowledge. Maybe his instinctive sensitivity is constantly picking up on what his subconscious is trying to tell him.

How can this work between us, with so much that can't be said or discussed? How far am I allowed to go before there is a consequence? As my mentor warned, I will then have to handle any changes that occur as a result of my actions. I've been talking Alex into believing that we can be together and make a future where we can become more than the sum total of two individuals. Am I now the one backing away? Does Alex sense that this morning? In fairness to us both, I need to think this through a little before I say anymore. I wonder, fleetingly, if the tables have turned. Am I in danger of altering Alex's future, robbing him of his true destiny in this life if I don't let him go? I wonder why we feel such a strong bond, which on one level feels so right yet on another so wrong.

"What? What are you thinking? Don't hide your feelings from me Ceri, that's all I ask. I'm sorry I panicked, that's all it was. You are right. Ethan's theory is only a theory."

"Let's take each day as it comes. Try not worry too much about tomorrow for the moment. I'm feeling a little off-colour today…"

"Hey angel," I love the sense of warmth in his voice as he says that word, "you *are* my angel, Ceri, beyond any shadow of a doubt. We've been through a lot and now it's our turn to grab some happiness. The thought of losing you completely scared me, even though it was due to my own stupidity." He places his hand on my cheek, his eyes gazing into mine as if he's searching for something. "Look, I'm going to be late if I don't leave for work. We'll talk about what happened when I get home tonight. Please try to have a relaxing day, you look really tired. I'll pick up something for that sore throat. See you later." He stoops to kiss me, lingering a moment to look at me before pulling away. "I never dared to dream this day would come. You'll still be here when I get back this evening, won't you?"

It's an attempt at humour that has a hollow ring to it: he's scared I'll change my mind.

"Of course, now go! You can't be late for work and I mustn't laze around all day. I need to start job hunting. I'll be here, promise!"

He turns to face me with the biggest smile on his face and a little thrill courses through my body. As I watch him walk away, I notice that what I always thought of as a sashay was really almost a dancer's glide. I believed Alex wasn't interested in women in general, but I'm beginning to see that it was his inherent sensitivity that helped reinforce my opinion. He's tall, slim and lean, his body isn't overly-developed but it's well defined. The way he walks lends an air of femininity and, because his face is so perfect, there's a sense of him not being quite real. Oh, listen to me! I can see inside him and I know the goodness and selflessness within his core, it's just unusual for the outside to match the inside. Before my trip back to the ethereal world, if anyone had asked me what a reincarnated angel looks like, I would have given Alex as an example. Thinking about myself, I feel I probably present as someone who is rather nervous and often prefers their own company.

A loud "Huh," escapes my lips. No one in their right mind would guess I was the angel. What I'm wondering is, how long would Alex have continued to live the life of a monk, hung up because he was in love with me but too scared by his dreams to say anything? His love has a depth that is way above his vibration level. It's an emotion that I invoke within him and I know beyond a shadow of a doubt that it exists within me too.

Chapter Five – A Friend In Need

I spend the morning phoning a few contacts, getting the word out that I'm looking for a job. Fortunately I know a lot of people in the business and losing my job with Portingale & Hughes Advertising isn't quite the disaster I thought it would be. No one asks why I left, and I draw the conclusion that most people in the business have heard about Mason Portingale's reputation. It's well known that he isn't an easy man to work for, although I wonder too if people sense he can be an outright bully at times.

Sheena arrived back in the UK yesterday and sent me a text suggesting we meet up. I'm longing to see her, but also worried that she'll notice a change in me. She knows me better than anyone else, aside from my brother Seb, and this is a big test. Seb is still travelling; it's his way of coming to terms with the sudden death of Anna on their wedding day. My instincts tell me he will eventually return, but not until he has worked through his grief in the only way that makes sense to him. He's flitting about from country to country, his adrenalin junkie days firmly behind him now. Instead he's using that energy to help people in need, as a volunteer. He's in Cambodia at the moment, helping to build a new water course. His emails are merely a line or two, he doesn't share much information and I know he's simply letting me know he's safe.

Not having him around makes Sheena's presence even more important. She's my family when Seb isn't here. I only wish my parents could live with the fact that I'm so very different to Seb. He was the easy child and I was the black sheep. I doubt that will ever change.

We meet up at Starbucks and I'm running late, so Sheena is already in the queue when I arrive. We grab our lattes and manage to find a small corner table.

"What's up?" She eyes me suspiciously, probably assuming I've had one of my psychic episodes.

"There's been a development." I feel a little awkward, not knowing where to start.

"Spill the beans." She slips off her coat and leans across to give me a big hug. The instant we touch it's like someone freezes the frame: that one moment appears to have stalled both time and movement. The seconds tick by and yet nothing moves. I break away, feeling as if someone has knocked the wind out of me.

Then I see her.

Kelly is here, as if she hadn't died four years ago and is joining us for coffee today. Sheena is busy folding her coat and trying to find space under the table to accommodate her over-sized bag. In that split second I understand. Kelly has always been around Sheena, I just couldn't see her before. She's one of Sheena's guardian angels. I shake my head, trying to clear my thoughts as Sheena peers across the table at me.

"What's up? You look like someone just walked over your grave." Her voice snaps me back. I have to pull myself together.

"I'm coming down with something. I have a really sore throat…" the words die in my mouth as it becomes dry with anxiety. Kelly is standing a mere two feet away and appears as real as any of the other people in the café. In fact, that isn't quite right. She appears *more* real and they are simply a paler backdrop.

"Poor you, I hope it isn't so bad that you can't tell me all your latest news." Sheena adds sugar to her coffee, totally oblivious to the fact that Kelly is with us and for the first time in four years our little trio is reunited. I want to reach out and touch Kelly, to convince myself she's real and yet I know she's only here in spirit. Presenting to me, I swear, dressed as she was the last time I saw her. That was before the leukaemia had weakened her body and begun to claim her life. Tears gather in my eyes and Sheena is now staring at me.

"Ceri, what's wrong?"

Should I tell her about Kelly? Accepting my gift is one thing; understanding that everyone has a link with the other side is another. I don't want to frighten her.

"Alex is back in my life." I'd intended to tell her anyway and I only hope she thinks the tears are because I'm emotional.

"Well, I'm not surprised exactly, although the guy really hurt you. I've never known you to run away from any situation before, but the way he talked to you was unforgiveable. Is it going to be a permanent thing?" Her concern is tangible; she's looking out for my interests and thinks Alex might hurt me again. Kelly hasn't moved: her image isn't quite so sharp now but it's comforting to know she's there, listening.

"I think so. He stayed last night. He wants me to tell him about what happened while we were apart, hoping we can move on. I convinced him he has nothing to worry about and that we can be together."

"Then what's worrying you?" Sheena looks at life in a black and white way and I'm not sure she'll understand.

"What if I'm wrong?"

"Well, you've known him for a little over two years. Considering you were so convinced he wasn't into women at all, I think that says he isn't fickle. I doubt many men would stand by nursing a broken heart and sitting alongside the one they love at work day in, day out. I'd say he has commitment, although I'm puzzled by the things he said to you when he lashed out. It struck me as a little out of character at the time."

"I don't mean I'm concerned about his motives. What about mine?"

Sheena raises her eyebrows.

"What have I missed? When you joined me in France to get away from everything you never mentioned ulterior motives. I know you Ceri, you don't play with people. You love him. Hook, line and sinker." She shrugs, obviously puzzled.

"But what if," I look around and lower my voice, conscious too that Kelly hasn't moved, "I'm using him. He's the first guy I've found that didn't back off the moment he found out that I see spirits. Quite the reverse, he's been a tower of strength. He had a mild interest in the subject, as many do, but after I left he read a book I gave him and then met up with the author."

"Really? Well, doesn't that prove he has your best interests at heart? That's a good thing, isn't it?"

"But the guy he saw said we shouldn't be together. He's a medium and spiritual teacher; I've read most of his books. Remember I told you that Alex was holding back because he kept having this dream about me? It seemed to be warning him to keep his distance, but also encouraging him to help me. Every time he drew close to me on an emotional level, his dream showed something bad happening to me. Ethan channelled a message and he told Alex we aren't meant to be together. I'm not Alex's life-partner."

I can't be any clearer and Sheena sits back, slightly open-mouthed.

"Rubbish, we make our own destiny." She looks a little annoyed. "Okay, I accept you see the other side but come on Ceri, a dream is just a dream. If it's repetitive then surely it's a hang up he has or some old memory about something unpleasant coming back to him. I doubt an hour goes by without you being in his thoughts, so they become tangled. Goodness, I dreamt about that guy from the latest James Bond movie last night, although that could be classed as more of a fantasy I suppose." Her gaze moves around the room and I wonder if she can see or sense that Kelly is here.

21

She's never mentioned anything and I'm pretty sure I'd be the first one Sheena would consult.

"I feel like I'm trapping him. And what if we commit and then it falls apart?"

"Welcome to the real world. I live it each day," she mutters. "Look, I've spent my entire adult life looking for Mr Right and there have been a lot of Mr Wrongs. He's a dish, Ceri, he says he loves you and you believe him. I know how you feel about him, so for goodness sake lighten up. Stop looking for reasons not to commit, you'll make me think this is really about you being scared of having a real, meaningful relationship."

We move on to talk about Sheena's time in Germany and the next project on the horizon. She's been asked to accompany a business man on a buying trip to Italy. He's in the antiques trade and he's mega rich and, allegedly – her words, very handsome and dazzling company. I asked how she could possibly know that and she said she read all about him in one of the latest celebrity gossip magazines.

"Are you sure this is a translation job and not an escort service?" I can't help myself laughing and then I notice that Kelly has disappeared. I stop mid-laugh and stare at the empty space.

"I probably shouldn't ask, but are you having one of your psychic moments?" Sheena's voice breaks into my thoughts.

"No, I just realised something about myself, that's all," I hedge. I can feel that Kelly is happy to be around Sheena to help and there is no need for any explanation of the role she's playing in her life. I send her a virtual hug, knowing that she'll feel it and appreciate our ethereal link.

"Well, stop being a drag and looking for the down side of everything. It's a trend you seem to be following more and more these days. Let Alex brighten up your life and go for it, lady!"

It hit me that the moment Sheena and I hugged, I could see with a clarity I didn't have before. Kelly has obviously always been around her. But when I'm close to Alex I can't sense anything. I can see his aura, his energy and the goodness in him, but whatever links he has to the ethereal plane are hidden from me. Is that what mortal loves does? Invoke some invisible wall through which the future can't be glimpsed?

Sheena leans forward, placing her hand over my arm.

"Take a little bit of advice, Ceri, meant in the spirit of sisterhood love. You have always felt you were unloveable, mainly because you never fitted in when you were younger either with your parents or your peers. Let go of it, don't carry that scar around with you and let it influence the rest of your life. You are a catch and Alex is an extremely lucky man. Heck, if you don't want him, throw him my way."

Chapter Six – Coming Clean

"Hi, my little angel." Alex wraps his arms around me and squeezes, then kisses the top of my head. He doesn't let me go, but rocks gently back and forth on the balls of his feet. "Oh, this feels so good, coming home to my woman."

I can't help myself as I burst out laughing. He sounds like the hunter-gatherer, home from a hard day's work. He sniffs the air and I look at him quizzically.

"I love a woman who can cook for her man and yet the house smells as fresh as if she hasn't lifted a wooden spoon or boiled a pan of water. Now that's what I call skill." He smirks.

"Could be because this woman has nothing planned for dinner and hasn't even given it a thought."

He feigns a sad face and, catching my hand, spins me around. "Then I'll take you out to dinner, or would you prefer takeaway?"

His happiness is infectious, but the last thing I feel like is getting ready to go out. "Takeaway?"

He nods. "Glad you said that. It wouldn't be so easy to talk in a public place. I don't want to force you though, if you'd rather not tell me where you went and what you did when we were apart."

He follows me into the sitting room, shedding his coat, tie, and shoes as we walk. In true Alex style he gathers them up in his arms and places them neatly on one end of the sofa. He proceeds to undo the cuffs of his shirt and roll his sleeves up to just below the elbow. He flashes those sexy wrists with absolutely no understanding of the way he's making my stomach flip. He unfastens the top two buttons of his shirt and collapses in the chair opposite me.

"What a day," he groans, shifting his body to sink back into the cushions.

"Okay, you go first. How was your day?" I ask. He reaches up to massage the back of his neck with his right hand, those sexy wrists calling out to me.

"Busy. It's very different to Portingale and Hughes, that's for sure. No sleazy Mason hanging around making everyone's life unbearable. But they don't have enough staff for the amount of work coming in. I'm not sure they can afford to take on anyone else, but I was thinking, should I ask on your behalf?"

"No, I'll be fine. I've made some calls today and something will turn up." I smile at him encouragingly. It's about time I did lighten up, as Sheena put it, and show Alex there is a fun side to me too.

"I'm glad you mentioned that. How do you feel about us moving in together? We already know each other pretty well. It's not as if we've just met. I like to think that the two years we've spent working so closely together would have shown up any disgusting habits either of us might have. I'm house-trained too." He looks nervous, hesitant and stupidly boyish for a guy his age.

"I know. It's one of the things I admired about you from the start." I try not to laugh. What I'm really thinking is that it was one of the things that made me think he wasn't into women. I've never known a man who pays so much attention to his personal grooming and is even tidier than I am.

"I've been mulling it over, and stop me if I'm running before I can walk here…" He jumps up and comes over to sit at my feet, placing one arm around my legs. It's a curious gesture, intimate without being overtly sexual. Loving. "But it would take the pressure off you having to find something straight away. We could rent out one of the apartments to bring in an income. Ceri, I don't want to push you into anything you don't feel comfortable with, but I feel I've wasted two years of our relationship by holding back and I'm not prepared to do that anymore."

I lean over him, sliding my fingers through the hair at the back of his head and down to rest my hand on his shoulder. The warmth of his skin through his shirt tells me his body chemistry is working overtime. The feel of him is strong and slightly tense.

"That's a great idea. I want this as much as you do, Alex, and I'm sorry I ran away. I guess you weren't the only one who was scared. I met up with Sheena today and she told me a few home truths. It made a lot of sense. I have to let go of the past and keep my sights firmly on the future."

He turns to kneel next to me, his lips brushing mine with a gentleness that's touching. He's a man who understands there are times for passion and times for loving reassurance. We're going to take this one step at a time.

***

We talked for hours, stopping only to take delivery of the Chinese takeaway, fill our plates, and to open a bottle of California's finest White Grenache. The alcohol wasn't necessary and we drank slowly, neither of us wanting to dull our senses. I recount the story of what happened after our argument. I told Alex about dashing off to France and meeting up with Sheena, about spending time on the coast and the long walks, during which I made myself face up to a lot of things that weren't easy to think about. I told him that while he sought advice from Ethan Morris, I turned to Mark Kessler. Alex hadn't heard about him, even though he's a celebrated local and an acclaimed psychic medium. He's also a motivational speaker. He travels all over the UK and his events are always sold out. I explained that I'd followed his website blog for a while and read some of his books. I went to one of his talks and afterwards

I hung around to buy one of his motivational CDs. We began chatting and I signed up for a meditation tutorial. Mark and I connected immediately and I worried that Alex might misinterpret that, but he seemed fine with it. When I explained that Mark had offered to mentor me, the only thing he said was, "If you trust him, I trust your judgement".

I had to admit there were a lot of similarities in Ethan and Mark's beliefs, but on the one occasion Alex had taken me to meet Ethan I felt a strange sense of being frowned upon. As if he was judging me and found me lacking in some way. Mark might not have quite so much experience, but he's the sort of person you can discuss something with and he will listen. He takes time to consider the point you are making and is happy to discuss anything at all. I think that was what was wrong. Ethan obviously felt he knew exactly what was what and Mark saw everything as not necessarily being written in stone.

That was then, of course, and this is now. Meeting up with Mark for my next session will tell me a lot more, now that I can see things more clearly. I am worried that it will change the way I view him, but there are so few options open to me. At the time I was hoping Mark would help me hone my skills. Now, I need him to introduce me to the psychic community so I can begin my new task. I have to do that in a way that will not make it obvious something has changed. For now it's enough that Alex simply accepts, without question, things he doesn't fully understand. It's another reason why I love him so much. People are so judgmental at times and it's a trait that can seriously undermine a person's confidence. No wonder so many people are now opening their eyes and thinking less about the material things in life and more about the spiritual aspect. There's a global sense of change. You can almost hear the cry gathering momentum…

There has to be more to life than this.

Chapter Seven – Heaven Or Hell

As an angel I know there is no heaven or hell, there is only creation and everything that exists within it. Hell is a state of mind which exists only on this plane. It manifests itself in different ways. Lower vibrations – young souls with little experience – often flounder, trapped and unable to let go of whatever holds them back on their journey to the ethereal plane. On earth they busy themselves with causing mischief. They often do a lot of damage as they impede the work done by higher energies: those who are here trying to help people find their spiritual pathway. Unfortunately they cause serious confusion by sending out messages that have no meaning at all. In time they do move on. These are often the spirits that ghost hunters find, as few of the higher energies are disposed to help those who cannot believe without having proof.

However, I wasn't prepared for the very real sense of over-whelming happiness that I'm feeling now I'm with Alex. I was happy doing the work I did, but this is something completely different. I can't liken it to anything I have ever experienced before. We have a sense of oneness that takes my breath away. I trust Alex implicitly and when I'm with him I am a better person. Not just happier and more content, but complete and able to give more of myself to him and my ethereal life as well.

The passion is beyond giving; it's a fusion. It begins as a

sensation of warmth, like basking in the sun on a glorious day, and ends with an explosion that takes me to another place. Somewhere that only Alex and I can go together. A place I've never been before, and at last I know what the word *love* really means. My previous experiences were nice, nothing more and nothing less. With Alex it has meaning, strength, and if there is a heaven then I'm in it now.

Something makes me stir and I roll away from Alex, turning onto my side. A chill hits me like a blast of icy cold air coming in through an open window on a winter's day. But I'm exhausted and my eyes are so heavy they won't stay open, no matter what my senses are telling me.

I drift into an uneasy sleep.

***

I awaken in the early hours of the morning, a cold sweat slick on my skin. I jump out of bed before I even have a chance to consider that I might disturb Alex. I hurry into the sitting room and open the laptop. The garish light from the screen blinds my sleepy eyes.

To: seb789@aol.com
Subject: Urgent
Message: Are you there? I need to speak to you. Please. Ceri xxxx

I look at the screen that confirms my message has been sent. A minute passes, then ten minutes, and my arms start to feel chilled. My phone vibrates and scuttles towards me across the desk top. As I reach for it, a tingle runs up my arm. The caller ID says *Seb*. My heart races. This is the first time I've spoken to him since Anna's death.

"Seb, are you okay?" The words come out in a rush.

"I don't know. I think I might be having some sort of nervous breakdown. I need to talk to someone I can trust, how did you know?" He sounds dispirited, isolated. Almost confused.

"I'm here and I'm listening." I can hardly keep the waver out of my voice. I want my brother to be here with me, not in some distant country that I'll never see. It's been too long. My instincts are screaming out *beware, tread carefully* and I wonder if he's been kidnapped or something. Life in Cambodia is hard, a strange mix of third world and modern life running in parallel. A few moments elapse and now I'm scared he's been involved in an accident. In his last email he briefly mentioned getting around in a tuk tuk. I Googled it and the examples that came up all looked like death-traps for the crazily busy roads. One feature I read said that traffic congestion in Phnom Penh was approaching a crisis.

"I… umm… don't know where to begin." He stops and there's a strange noise, then another, and it's clear he's sobbing. My stomach is churning and all of my senses seem to be kicking off all over the place. Whatever is behind this, I have to be careful about what I say.

"That's okay." I manage to keep my voice level and calm. "We all have moments where it's hard to find the words we need. Can I call you back? Are we in danger of getting cut off?" I'm unsure of his situation with regard to money, or whether he even has a mobile phone of his own now. I begin to panic. If we are cut off I feel a life-line is going to be severed.

"No, no. I have credit. I've been earning some money. It's good to hear your voice. I don't know why I didn't call you before." Another sob and the silent minutes pass, something deep down telling me to be patient and listen.

He lets out an anguished "Aaarghh," and I realise he's trying to pull himself together.

"Sorry Sis, I have good days and bad ones. Today has been bad, that's when I miss you the most. I'm not angry anymore. I mean, about losing Anna. I don't understand it, but I'm no longer in denial. Shit happens, life is unfair sometimes. No point in asking why Anna or why me? Feels like I'm trying to shift the pain onto someone else's shoulders and I'm past that point now. Only I thought I was coping and now I know I'm not."

I don't jump in to answer him. Instead I wait a few seconds to see if he's going to continue. He remains silent and I soften my voice, hoping he'll feel the healing vibes I'm sending along with my words.

"I know Seb, it's so hard to bear and it doesn't make any sense. I wish you were here, you sound like you need a hug."

He makes a noise that sounds like a laugh and a sob combined. "Yeah, I thought I was coping until this morning." More silence.

"What happened? You know you can tell me anything."

Several more minutes elapse.

"I saw Anna last night."

I wait, with bated breath, wondering if he'll continue.

"She leant over me. I had just woken up. Or maybe I was still asleep. I don't know, it's not clear. How can I have seen her? She spoke to me, looked me in the eyes and said 'Don't give up', and I cried out. Then she was gone. She was real, at the time I really believed that, but then she was gone – as suddenly as she had appeared."

His words come tumbling out and I struggle to keep up with him. His emotions are all over the place, one moment reflecting desperation and the next sounding hopeful.

"You did the right thing calling me. Where are you?"

"In the commune. It's basic but we have everything we need. The new irrigation system is nearly finished."

"Okay, you need hot, sweet tea or very strong coffee. Do you have access?"

"Yes."

"Good. Are you on a mobile or land line?"

"Mobile, it's mine. My old one was stolen. This is a cheap one I picked up."

"Okay, talk as you walk. Go make yourself something hot and strong."

I question Seb to keep him talking as he walks, about his

surroundings and the people he shares with. His voice returns to a more normal level and I'm relieved as that frantic edge gradually subsides. I can hear him clattering about as he brews his tea. He walks back to his room and then I ask him to describe it.

"It's a box really, very small. Only a single bed, one cabinet and a small window. The walls are a dirty grey and the floor is permanently dusty. The road outside isn't made up, but compacted dirt. I have a red flower, in a glass jar. I bought it this morning," he sobs uncontrollably. I sit through the worst five minutes of my life, listening to the heart-wrenching sound. "I bought it for Anna, after last night."

I hear some gulps and assume he's drinking the tea. After a few more minutes he begins talking again.

"Ceri, when someone is dead, they are dead. Anna no longer exists and I know that. But she was here and I don't think it was a dream." It sounds more like a challenge than a statement. "Why did you email me tonight of all nights?" The tone is accusatory.

"It isn't anything I've done Seb, but I felt something was wrong and that's why I made contact. She didn't choose to visit me. Anna is worried about you and it would have taken a considerable amount of effort for her to appear, even briefly. It's too soon, her energy levels will still be depleted as the transition between planes is draining."

"How can you say that so calmly? This is in my head. All in my head!" He shouts so loudly I have to hold the phone away from my ear.

"Seb, calm down. Drink your tea. This is a blessing. You have to see it for what it is: a message that shows you how much Anna still loves you. I know you don't believe in life after death, or any of the spiritual stuff," I have to pause for a moment to wipe away my own tears, "but your denial doesn't change the fact that it does exist. You are my precious twin brother and I can't lie to you just to help you make some sense of this. I also wouldn't mislead you. Anna is obviously worried about how you are coping, so what's really going on here?"

"I nearly did it, Ceri, nearly had the guts to end it all. The tablets started sliding down too easily, then the alcohol, and it felt so right. The promise of an end to the pain was enticing. Then I drifted off and suddenly Anna was there. I thought at first it was the curtain next to the window, shimmering in the moonlight. Then I realised there is nothing up to the window and suddenly Anna was standing there. She was frowning and I shrieked so hard my throat constricted. I threw up everywhere and then I cried. I was back to square one and I'm not sure I have the courage to go through with it again..."

***

We talked for over an hour and after he disconnected I sat there for a few moments, staring at the phone. Then I sobbed. For Anna, for Seb, and for myself. What a mess this life was turning out to be. As twins, does this mean that both of our futures are destined to be blighted? Our soul mates paraded before us, only to be snatched away by death and, in my case, by the fear of ruining Alex's life?

Two hours later I received an email from Seb:

You saved me from myself Ceri. Is that what a twin with sensitivity does? Live their life half-feeling what the other feels? Because you sure know what's in my heart and in my mind. Seb xx

Chapter Eight – Earthbound

The weekly session I have booked with Mark Kessler tonight ties my stomach up in knots. It will be the first time I've seen him since I was called back.

The sense of duality I have isn't quite what I was expecting. I can see auras quite clearly now and sense the nature of the energy that lies deep within people. It isn't simply an intuitive thing, but a tangible sense of knowing. I no longer seem to have déjà vu incidents as I'd had before. What will tonight's session bring? Will I feel any differently towards Mark once I see him? This morning I asked Alex if he wanted to come along with me. He said he would have loved to come, but he's showing someone around his apartment and won't be back until late. I wondered if he purposely booked the appointment to coincide with my session to give me some space. I appreciate the thought. He doesn't want me to feel that he's watching all the time and it's his way of letting me know that he trusts me.

There's another email from Seb this morning.

She came to visit me again. I'm beginning to understand why you believe what you do, but this isn't for me, Ceri. I can't accept that she's not here and yet she's around me. I did a very stupid thing and I'm sorry about that, I've put it behind me. I just can't believe in something that doesn't make any sense. Don't worry about me, I'm moving on and I'll keep myself active. No more wallowing.

Seb xx

It was a relief knowing that the worst was over. Seb was going to go through a time of change in the way he thinks and what he believes. He's on his own spiritual journey and eventually he will come home. After all this time of not knowing what would happen next, I offered up a silent prayer as I closed the email. I paused for a few moments, eyes closed and I saw a picture in my mind. I've never been to Cambodia, but suddenly I was there with him. The reality of experiencing the sights and sounds, the smells and a sense of disorganised chaos, was a shock. I came back with a jolt, wishing that Seb was here. I know it's not in his fate to permanently return to what would be, to him, a mundane life in this country. I think about his guardian angels and ask them to protect him while he seeks to find some sort of inner peace.

My phone kicks into life, disturbing my thoughts. It's Mark, and I wonder if he can sense my anxiety.

"Hi, Mark." I feel awkward, dreading that he'll know I'm not the same person and want to know the reason for the change in me.

"Ceri, sorry to interrupt, but the session I had booked before yours has been cancelled. If you are free, we could get together earlier. I'm here all afternoon."

"Yes, great. I was just about to organise my CV, so no great excitement there. I'll be with you in twenty minutes."

I run a brush through my hair, put on a smear of lipstick, and grab my coat and bag on the way out. I stop by the door and leave a note for Alex.

Gone to Mark's earlier than planned so we can eat together, see you tonight. Fingers crossed for the apartment. Love you, C xx

Out in the open it's nice to fill my lungs, even if there is just a faint whiff creeping into the air from the car engines ticking over as they wait for the traffic lights to change. I walk quickly, deep in thought. What do I say to Mark? While I have knowledge now, I still don't understand the practical application of how it works on this level. Seeing the good and bad in people is one thing, understanding how to interact and use what I know is another. I'm rather embarrassed when I almost collide with a little old lady. I'm not sure whether she noticed me walking towards her, head down and mind elsewhere. Suddenly she's immediately in front of me and I let out a "sorry" as I quickly side-step to avoid bumping into her. We are both a little shaken and I reach out to take her elbow and steer her towards the low wall alongside the pavement. The moment my hand connects a bright light, similar to a streak of lightning, zips up into the air. I fall back slightly and she looks at me quizzically.

"Are you all right my dear?" Her voice is very genteel and soft.

"Yes, I'm fine, but I'm so sorry I nearly ploughed straight into you." I indicate for her to sit down and we both perch on the low wall.

"Bad day?" she asks, as if we haven't just avoided colliding but are chatting over a cup of tea.

"No, a lot going on in my head and I really do need to look where I'm going. I'm very sorry that I didn't see you until the last minute."

As I give her a reassuring smile to check that she isn't as shaky as I feel, a young woman walks towards us. She extends her arm in a half-wave.

I'm about to acknowledge her when I realise this is a spirit. She wants me to pass on a message, but all I have so far is her presence. She stands there smiling at me and the sensation of pure love emanating from her makes me tearful.

"How are you feeling?" I place my hand on the old lady's arm and give a little squeeze.

"I'm fine. I wasn't looking where I was going either." She has a soft, high-pitched laugh that is almost a girly-giggle. "It's such a pity the traffic is so heavy nowadays," she murmurs.

The young woman has moved closer, she's within reach. She keeps looking at me intently, as if she's encouraging me to say something, but I have no idea what she wants.

"Bide a while." The words come out gently and I have no idea where they're from. It's not a phrase I've ever used before. "Sit and remember."

"How lovely." The old lady looks up at me with sparkling eyes. "My daughter used to say that. I do want to sit and remember, often, but it's still too painful. Is she wearing a red woollen coat and black shoes?" She looks hesitant, glancing across at me nervously. "I'm not sure she's safe, you see, and I need to know it's really her," she whispers, leaning in anxiously as if she might be overheard. There is no one else around.

I notice that the young woman is now stooping and draping her arms around the old lady's shoulders. Instinctively I pull back, although there's plenty of space between us.

"She's safe and she's here. Yes, her coat is red and it has a heavy weave. She's wearing black leather boots though." Tears fill my eyes. The old lady reaches across to pat my hand as the young woman pulls away.

She's gone.

"That's her." The old woman's words are barely audible and I strain to catch them. "Thank you, my dear." Her voice is overcome with emotion.

We sit in silence for several minutes, her hand still placed over mine. Her fingers are cold. She reaches up to adjust the little brown hat perched on her head and smiles. I stand up and offer her my arm; she leans on me heavily to pull herself up, although she's so slight there's hardly any weight. With a little wave the old lady turns and walks away.

I almost run the rest of the way to Mark's, trying not to dwell on the strong emotions hovering around me. I can't do this, I can't do this. How can I survive if I feel everyone's deepest, darkest hurt as soon as I meet them? I'm shaking as I ring the bell and when Mark opens the door he can see something is up.

"Hi Ceri, that was a long twenty minutes. Are you okay? Come in."

Mark helps me take off my coat and suggests we have coffee first, so I follow him into the kitchen. He can see I'm a little shaken and he's giving me some breathing space. He makes polite conversation, telling me about his son and a football match he has coming up. Then I follow him through to his consulting room. It's a large, ground floor room that looks out onto a stunning garden. The grass is perfectly manicured and there is an abundance of flowers and shrubs. Quite simply it's a haven, and each time I come here I feel a sense of calm wash over me.

"Rough morning?" He gives me a few minutes to settle into the chair and tuck my bag to one side.

"Weird morning." I put my head down and stare into my coffee cup.

"An experience?"

I don't want to look at him because he presents very differently now. His aura is like a shiny gold band radiating out from him.

"Ceri, has anything unusual happened since I saw you last? Whatever you tell me is in confidence, but I have to ask... can you see my aura?"

I nod.

"Ah," he mutters, letting out a deep breath, "I thought something had changed. It's nothing to worry about. It happens sometimes, although it can take a while to become used to it. What do you see?"

"A gold band. It's very clear." I can't see any reason not to be honest with him. I can only hope he doesn't question me any further.

"That's good. Thank you. Gold reflects spiritual energy, that's a great compliment. Do you want to know the colour of your aura? Because it has changed since I last saw you."

Our eyes lock and a moment of recognition passes between us, before I avert my gaze.

"It's bright emerald green. It was a pale yellow the last time we met."

"Which means?" I have no idea what the relevance of each colour has, and wish I'd thought to research it beforehand.

"Well, you were an emerging energy, excited about new ideas, the changes to come. Your awareness has moved on and now you have the ability to be a healer. You are also love-centred, it's amazing. I can't believe the change in you."

I'm relieved he's regarding it as normal progression. I have no idea how frequently the colours of the aura change. I know the state of one's health affects it and I'm only too glad that he doesn't seem to want to dig any deeper.

"It's good, and you must remember that it's not my job to pry, only to assist you. I thought we'd talk about chakras today. The greater your understanding becomes, the more effective you will be in opening up and closing down when meditating. It's important to acquire a discipline that you adhere to every single time you meditate. Leaving yourself open, as it's referred to, will mean that lesser energies will be attracted to you."

I place the empty cup on the side table and settle back in my chair. "Is that something I should worry about?" Of course, I know all about lesser energies, the mischief makers who toy with those who have no faith, no sense of belief. Those who seek to either discredit the spirit world, or see proof as profit.

"Our sessions will help you develop the focus and strict regime you need, so that you have a framework within which to operate. You will work at a higher level than is required for mediumship, even. My belief is that while it does serve a purpose, it's merely to give encouragement to people who are searching, mindful only that something is missing from their lives. A simple message from a loved one can be enough for some people to reach out for more information, and so their spiritual journey begins."

Mark stands, leaning across to grab my coffee mug and placing both of them on his desk. Then he takes a CD from a small stack in front of him and slides it into an open tray. Gentle music emits through the surround sound speakers and he turns the volume down very low.

Each session begins in the same way. I follow the example Mark sets as he adjusts his position. He straightens his back and draws himself up, as if someone is pulling an invisible thread above him. His feet are apart and flat on the floor, his arms loose in his lap, with palms open and fingers slightly curled. He arches his back for one moment and lowers his shoulders, taking a deep breath. In unison we breathe in through our noses and out through our mouths for a minute or two. The music is uplifting and my shoulders begin to feel lighter, all the tension in my muscles draining away.

***

An hour later I'm on my way home. Mark guided me through a much longer meditation this time. He took me to a woodland area and along a path. Someone was walking with me, but I couldn't recognise them as they kept to the edge of my peripheral vision. I only knew that it was an old friend and one of my spirit guides.

Afterwards Mark talked in depth about chakras and suddenly things seemed to slot into place. I immediately thought of Alex and made a mental note to talk to him about it tonight. I also told Mark about the old lady. I wanted to ask him about the spirit of her daughter. While I know so many things, there are lots of earth-bound traits that confuse me. I wanted to know why it was necessary for her to appear so clearly to me when the presence of her energy would have been enough. He explained that energy can choose to present itself in any way it pleases. The physical body only has relevance here on earth. So spirit presents in the form that will be most easily recognisable when described to the recipient of the message. It makes identification much easier and was one of the most effective forms of validation.

It made perfect sense, although a tinge of sadness hit me. I had a sudden longing for the ethereal plane. It's the place where energies exist, without form or substance. Being simply a vibration as intended and each unique in its own way. One thing I know for sure about life here on earth is that it's hard and I'm not surprised people often feel they have failed some sort of test.

Chapter Nine – In Love With Love

"Oh, you're back earlier than I thought. The viewing didn't go well?" I sidle up to Alex and cuddle into his back. He stirs something in a pan that smells of rich, buttery onions and tomatoes. I'm in for an Italian treat.

"On the contrary, we have a taker. I'm officially homeless as from next Saturday."

He lays the wooden spoon down on a piece of kitchen towel and spins around to draw me into his arms.

"Mmm… you taste nice!"

"You smell of garlicky onions," I laugh.

"How was the session with Mark?"

"Great, I learnt a lot about chakras."

"Well, grab the garlic bread and I'll dish up. If you can take the wine through I'll be there in a moment, can't wait to hear all about it."

Before he lets me go he kisses first one cheek, and then the other. His lips are warm and gentle.

"Let go of me then." I laugh and he squeezes a little tighter before releasing me. "I'm starving."

I have to admit that Alex's cooking is rather good. His attention to detail in all things means that, while it's simple, the taste reflects the effort he has put into the dish.

"Is it good?" he asks, almost as soon as I pop a forkful into my mouth.

"Mmm. Delicious! I wish you would cook all the time." I give him my best persuasive smile.

"A smile alone won't do it," he returns suggestively. His eyes linger for a few moments, as if he's seeing me for the first time. I feel my cheeks colouring up. "Tell me about Mark." He returns to his pasta, expertly winding his linguini around his fork.

"We did a woodland walk. I wasn't alone, but whoever was with me didn't come forward. I think it might have been my grandmother. I had a distinct sense of recognition. I thought I smelt her perfume…"

"Wow, that's a result. Perhaps I should try meditating, you can teach me."

It's wonderful to be able to talk to Alex about anything and everything. I reach out and slide my hand over the back of his neck, giving him an affectionate squeeze.

"I found out something about you, too."

He looks up as I pull my hand away. "You can't see all my secrets… can you?"

"No, nothing like that. It's to do with your chakras and your traits."

"Oh, the vibes that made you think I wasn't into women. Ceri, that doesn't do much for my self-esteem as a guy women find irresistible. Maybe that's why I've never had much luck on the dating front."

"Well, for a start I'm rather glad about that and secondly, your problem is that you are just too darned good looking. Women feel a bit intimidated chatting up a guy who looks like every woman would fall at his feet. No, it's about your attention to detail."

"Tell me more. What exactly are chakras, I've heard the term but I'm not sure I understand what it's all about."

"Well, there are seven major chakras within the body and these are the energy centres. Opening them up allows a flow into and out of the aura. Mark explained to me that, equally as important as the opening up process to be receptive and reach a state of oneness, is the closing down process." I stop for a moment to scoop up some linguine and gauge Alex's reaction.

"Yeah, I've read a little and it's something to do with attracting negative energy or something, am I right?"

"Spot on. Lower astral energies, the ones who mislead and have nothing better to do. It's important to heed the balance within ourselves as it aligns the physical with the emotional and mental aspects of the life force. The seven points run in a line up through our bodies, ending with the crown chakra on the top of the head. Each is like a flower head with petal-like openings, invisible to most of us but energy workers can see them.

"What I didn't appreciate was that our surroundings can indicate when we have a problem with a blockage in any of our energy centres. I immediately thought of you." I stop to take another mouthful of food and give him a mischievous smile.

He groans. "Am I the textbook example of a walking chakra disaster zone?" His eyes twinkle.

"Quite the reverse, actually. I've learnt that dirty window panes might indicate a clouded third-eye perception and a dusty, cluttered bedroom can indicate negativity in one's love relationship. It seems cleaning really is cathartic."

"Well, I think we'd better finish up here and go dust the bedroom. I wouldn't want anything to hold us back now we're finally living together under the same roof."

***

I love having Alex around and I miss him when he leaves for work. Suddenly the apartment feels empty because his energy tends to fill every little space. It's lovely to laze around together, often in bed, feeling warm and cuddly after the passion we share so easily and without reservation. Being able to let down my guard and be myself feels like coming home after a long time away. He doesn't probe and I'm surprised that it's easier than I thought it would be. Why was I so worried? When something is right there is a natural flow and things around us both are flowing perfectly. I'm loved and in love, what more could anyone ask for?

I've had two interviews this week and both resulted in a job offer. It seems the universe is smiling upon me. One was part-time work and after a chat with Alex we decided I should accept that offer. I can spend a little more time on my psychic abilities, and that's becoming increasingly important. Mark has asked me along to one of his workshops and if he feels I'm ready, he's going to encourage me to take an active part. It will only be a small group, so I think I'll feel comfortable putting myself out there.

For the first time since my return I feel that life on this plane has something special to offer. Something that is worth being here for, setting aside all of the negatives about how unkind people and life can be. I begin to see that it's about avoiding the pitfalls: all the negative stuff that's in the media, fuelling a general air of disillusionment. People give up on their dreams, dragged down by incidents that are of no consequence whatsoever. I'd never really understood the glass half full/glass half empty thing, but now I do. I've chosen to surround myself with Alex's positive attitude, and it rubs off. Less and less I notice the harsh, cruel side of this life and more and more I celebrate the positives. No wonder depression exists here on this plane: it's hard to disentangle yourself from things that constantly seek to drag you down. There is no hell, but people choose to put themselves into a kind of hell because they lose sight of what matters.

Then something clicks.

That's what I'm supposed to do! Encourage people to let go of their negativity and embrace the positive. Send out good karma and it comes back to you a thousand times over.

Chapter Ten – First Impressions

Seb has emailed a few times. He thinks he's making some sense of his life, although I fear he is still very vulnerable at the moment. He's with a group of people who sound like a weird religious sect, trying to isolate their members from the real world. I've expressed my concerns but can tell he has to go through this and come out the other side.

Don't lose touch Seb, whatever happens. I respect your choices, but keep an open mind, please. That's all I ask. I'm always here for you, if and when you want to talk. Ceri xxx

Alex knows that I'm worried and has tried to reassure me. What I can't tell him is that in my work on the ethereal plane I can see Seb and I know exactly what's happening. He's being led down a path by someone who claims to be a higher being, but who knows very little. He's the worst sort of believer: someone whose knowledge is minimal although his ego is large. This man thinks he's God, or the closest thing to him on this earth. Worshipping false idols comes to mind and whilst it's clear to me Seb isn't swallowing everything he's being told, he remains curious. I can only watch from a distance, but I'm prepared to step in if necessary.

I seem to be managing my two very distinct worlds effortlessly.

There doesn't seem to be any overlap and I don't think I've let anything slip.

"Are you ready yet?" Alex saunters into the bedroom and sashays towards me as if he's going to pounce.

"No, so don't come in here and start distracting me. I'm trying to do my make-up and I'll end up looking like a panda bear if I don't concentrate. I'm nervous. You can sit down and tell me some more about your boss if you want to help."

He sits on the edge of the bed, mindful not to upset the perfectly placed pillows, and I love that he cares about those little things. I never knew why ambience was so important, I simply knew it affected my mood and when everything was in order, I felt happier. After Mark's session on chakras it all became very clear. Cleanliness really is next to Godliness, and the reason is that dirt and clutter can stop the flow of energy. Since Alex moved in the apartment looks even better than it did before and, if that reflects our relationship, then this place is full of love and free-flowing energy.

"You know all about the company, Grey's Advertising, and Niall Grey is the kind of boss you'd stay late for to meet a deadline, even if he wasn't paying you. I've never met his wife but I assume they are going to be quite like-minded. There's no need to be nervous about meeting them," he's puzzled and concerned because I'm anxious.

"Technically I'm out of work, I'm a psychic and I'm not the usual sort of girlfriend someone would expect." I zip up my make-up case and choose some earrings. "How do I look?" I spin around for Alex to pass judgement.

"Bea-u-ti-ful. Much too attractive to take out on a work celebration dinner. You'll make Niall jealous." He gingerly places his arms around me. "I won't crush the dress," he murmurs into my hair. His body presses hard against mine and that little frisson of heat begins to flood through me.

"You're naughty, do you know that?" I turn my head, brushing my lips against his cheek. I move on to lightly tease his soft, gorgeous mouth. He kisses me back with a fierceness that makes me turn weak at the knees. I close my eyes and savour the moment, knowing full well any trace of lipstick will now have evaporated. I slide my arms down around his waist and Alex slides his hands down over my back, applying a slight pressure to pull my hips into him.

"I know, but you are just so, so sexy, Ceri. I can't keep my hands off you."

"I noticed," I reply, reluctantly pushing him away. I make my way to the bathroom to start again, brushing any vestiges of lipstick off my teeth. He follows close behind me and suddenly I'm in his arms, his body pressing mine up against the wall. I can't resist him and this moment is all that matters. Any thoughts about being late fade away.

***

"We're running a little late Niall, my apologies. This is my partner, Ceri Adams." Alex slides his arm out from around my waist. I step forward to shake first Niall's hand and then his wife's, as he turns to introduce her to us.

"Alicia, this is Alex Delano. Hello Ceri, lovely to meet you."

Niall walks around the table to pull out a chair for me. Alex has disappeared with our coats. I feel slightly panicky standing here on my own, so I paste on a big smile and concentrate on friendly eye contact. Niall's aura is orangey red. He's a confident and creative individual, although I doubt he'll be very interested in anything spiritual. Alicia's aura is a very dark grey and it isn't opaque, but quite a solid band of colour. That isn't good, it means she's holding onto fear and that is causing her some serious health problems. There's a large cluster of grey around her temples and I'm guessing she suffers from the most draining headaches. Maybe she has one coming now.

I look up from my thoughts, sensing I've missed something.

"I was asking what you would like to drink, Ceri."

Alex appears and answers for me as he settles into his chair. "Whatever you are having is fine for both of us," he says with a smile that looks a little forced. He looks nervously at Alicia and gives a little nod of acknowledgement, then back at me. Alex holds up my wine glass whilst Niall pours from a bottle sitting in a wine bucket on the table.

"Thank you." I take the glass Alex offers and raise it to toast both Niall's and Alicia's. Everyone is all smiles and I turn to Alex, to graze glasses. Something goes wrong and instead of a light touch, my glass shatters into a million pieces. Wine and shards of glass cascade down into my lap, making me jump. The look on his face startled me, something isn't right. Two waiters immediately come over and it's an embarrassing few minutes as they clear up the glass. Another waiter brings me some napkins to mop my dress and the table, then lays a new place setting.

"I'm so sorry, I don't know quite what happened," I'm mortified. "There really wasn't any reason why—"

"Faulty glass I suspect," Niall intercedes, obviously trying to make me feel better. Alex grabs my hand and gives it a gentle squeeze.

"One of those things, Ceri." He passes me the menu and there's a little light conversation about what to choose. It's a smart restaurant and very expensive, which makes this incident so much worse. I'm embarrassed and also confused about Alex. He's on edge and looks nervous. I wonder if he's disappointed in me and thinks I've let him down. I bite my lip, inwardly mad at myself for being so clumsy.

A waiter appears to take our order and things return to a more normal and relaxed atmosphere. I feel rather silly sitting here in a wine-splashed dress, only thankful that I wore black and it was white wine. The napkins mopped up most of it, but it's still damp in a couple of spots. A little wine goes a long way.

Thankfully the conversation begins to flow, dominated by the guys. Niall very kindly sings Alex's praises, which makes him squirm a little, and this time we air-kiss our glasses to toast Alex's promotion. Alicia says very little and only picks at her starter. The evening draws to a close very unexpectedly when Alicia suddenly turns very pale, as if she is going to faint. She admits to having the most awful migraine and virtually collapses, leaning into Niall, who puts a protective arm around her. He indicates for a waiter to bring the coats and begins apologising, insisting we stay to finish our meal.

It seems to have been a night of apologies, as we shake hands once more and bid each other goodnight.

Alex looks rather relieved as we make our way out of the restaurant a short while later, the evening in ruins.

Outside I can't help but ask the question. "What was that all about? For one moment you looked like you'd seen a ghost."

"It was nothing, you know me. I don't like attention and then when Niall started going on about my work… I'm just glad that's over. I'll be sure not to do anything to warrant another promotion," he adds, soberly.

"Well, when it comes to making a first impression, I think this is one evening we'll all want to forget!"

Chapter Eleven – A Little Doubt

Alex is rather subdued at breakfast the next morning and I'm wondering whether he's disappointed that last night ended up being a damp squib.

"Hey, I'm sorry about last night. I don't know quite what happened." My apology sounds pathetic.

"It's fine. Accidents happen. Socialising with the boss isn't a great idea, unless you get to sleep with her that is." He throws me a cheeky grin.

"Yes, but it spoiled your celebration. I'm so proud of you and I wanted it to go well."

"What was your initial impression? Any particular vibe you picked up?" He sounds casual, but there's an edge to his voice.

"No. Niall seemed like a nice guy. I couldn't really pick up very much from Alicia. I had the impression that she wasn't very well. I guess her migraine was hanging around from the start of the evening and that's what I could sense. She was pleasant enough, she laughed in all the right places before she began to feel really poorly."

"There's nothing for me to worry about then?"

I look up, wondering what prompted that strange question and why he's concerned.

"No, I don't think so. You aren't having second thoughts about

51

being with Grey's, are you?"

"I get on well with Niall. He's a workaholic and so am I, we understand each other, but I'll have to see how it goes. It might have been a mistake taking this promotion and if it is, then I'll look for another job."

I can feel something is bothering him although I have no idea what exactly, so I change the subject. "I'm looking forward to starting work next week. We've agreed on alternate days, Monday to Friday. I've spoken to Mark, so he knows I'm available to help out with any workshops on the two days I'm not working. I thought I'd keep the evening sessions to a minimum. I don't want it to eat into our time together any more than necessary."

The fact that Alex doesn't immediately look up reaffirms his head is somewhere else. I wonder if the job is stretching him a little too far. I know he's not comfortable managing staff and that it hasn't been easy for him. He's encountering a little resentment, because he hasn't been with Grey's very long and Niall selected him as the best candidate over some longer-term employees. I know Alex hates ill feeling of any kind. He's going to have to ride the storm until it settles down, and it will. I walk around to his side of the table and plant a kiss on his cheek.

"They'll all grow to love you, as I do." I inhale and close my eyes, mentally invoking every strand of healing within my body to surround him.

"I sincerely hope not! I've discovered having one woman in my life is difficult enough." His mood is lighter and he stands, turning to wrap me in a bear hug.

"What did I do before you came into my life? Nothing else seems to count for anything at all. This is only work we're talking about and I'm not a total wimp. So don't worry your gorgeous little head about it."

"Alex."

"Yes?"

"Guys don't say 'gorgeous', it's camp."

"Noted, boss." He tips me a salute and gives me his cheekiest grin.

ALEX

Chapter Twelve – Sometimes The Truth Isn't Pretty

I kiss Ceri, holding her for a little bit longer than necessary. Every time we part I worry that when I arrive home she won't be there. I know it's crazy. The reason she ran away before was because I said some awful things that weren't true. I was hurting, frustrated and desperate. It was hell being around her every day for two years, three months, and eight days without being able to acknowledge my love for her. Since she's been back and we've been together, everything is perfect. Until this damned promotion upset everything.

I keep walking, my head full of regrets, anger and desperation. What am I going to do? If Niall finds out that Alicia and I have a past together, I'm history. How will I explain that to Ceri? I hate lying to her – even if it is a lie by omission. But what can I say? Admitting the truth is going to be ugly and it was, but it sounds harsher when the words are spoken.

We were very young when we met and I really liked Alicia. We'd been seeing each other off and on for a couple of months when I received a phone call saying she was pregnant. She told me that she'd had counselling and was going to have an abortion. We were both in our first jobs after leaving university and the world stretched out enticingly before us. The news brought me down to earth with a bang. The day Alicia rang to tell me I was stunned, and I know she was struggling to hold it all together. We were dating exclusively but neither of us had said the word love, we weren't at that place. I can now see that we weren't ever going to fall in love. Not the sort of love I have for Ceri but, of course, you don't know that until you've experienced it for yourself.

There was no nastiness, no ugly scene, and that was the crazy part. When I said I would do whatever she wanted, that we could get married and somehow make it work, she laughed bitterly. "We can't even look after ourselves properly, what sort of parents would we make?" I hung my head in shame, thinking she was right and wondering how we could have been so careless.

We were just two young people who made the biggest mistake of all. I never saw her again after that. She refused to have anything to do with me. I tried to ring her several times, but it went to voicemail. Eventually a friend of hers sent me a text. She told me that if I had any respect for Alicia at all I would leave her alone and let her get on with her life. Alicia wrote me a letter a couple of months later, saying that we were both to blame and it was likely she would never forgive herself.

She was right in many ways, our relationship wouldn't have worked. We were too young to handle the situation. I've told Ceri everything about myself except this one thing. She's an angel and what the hell will she think of me if she finds out? I'm really scared that she can see inside of me, see what I'm hiding. I've been reading everything I can get my hands on to find out how it all works. Yes, a part of that is because I want to support her, but I'm running scared that my secret will be discovered.

I spoke to Ethan in a roundabout way and he says the rarity of an angel having an earthly life means it's difficult to imagine how that works. He believes that with lesser vibrations sent to this plane to help others, if they have an emotional attachment, it inhibits what they can see. But with angels, who knows? I've been working on the basis that Ceri would have said something by now, but I'm worried sick. If Niall had mentioned Alicia by name I might have caught on, but I still wouldn't have known it was her for sure, until last night.

I jump back as a car horn shatters my thoughts. I realise I'm stepping off the pavement and the crossing light is red. I'm anxious about seeing Niall today in case Alicia has said anything. A lot of couples share everything from the past before they make a firm commitment to each other. I know other people believe there's no point in raking over the details of old romances. Ceri's past was exactly as I expected. It made me feel sad to think that in the relationships she'd had the guys hadn't treated her with the respect she deserved. I know how much she loves me and how attracted to me she is, it shows in everything she does. She's a complex character, naturally, but there's an innocence and naivety to her nature that is refreshing. I understand the cautious side of her and I believe that's to do with her other-worldly connection. I never used to believe that there was more than one life, or one plane, but gradually I'm beginning to rethink the whole thing. At the moment I'm taking it all in my stride. People like Ethan, Ceri, and Mark are too intelligent to have the wool pulled over their eyes. Not only that, but I have my own gut feeling telling me that it's real, even though if someone asked me I couldn't explain it.

I'm beginning to wonder if a part of my desire to believe is because of that little soul, lost because Alicia and I had no relevant life experience and couldn't come to terms with what was happening. I should have done something, worked out a way to make it happen. I will admit, at the time, I was scared about the thought of providing a stable home environment for a baby and maybe also supporting a new wife. But it wasn't an empty offer, I would have managed somehow.

Niall and Alicia don't have children and I wonder if that was Alicia's choice? How can you think of bringing another baby into this world, when you failed to nurture a life that had begun to grow?

I have to shake myself and snap out of my reverie. I'm not in a fit state to walk through those office doors at the moment, pretending everything is fine. I need a large coffee with a couple of extra shots if I'm going to get through the day.

***

"Alex, hi. Thanks for coming in. Take a seat." Niall looks amiable, so I guess Alicia didn't say anything after all.

"Sorry about Alicia's headache, she suffers from these awful migraines. It's hormonal, you know how it is. It was great to meet Ceri. You're a very lucky man, Alex."

"Thanks, and I hope Alicia is feeling better today. It was a great meal and we both appreciated the gesture. Ceri felt awful about the glass."

"These things happen, probably some careless waiter not noticing a crack in the glass when they were laying the table. Poor Ceri, she handled it well and didn't make a fuss. I like that kind of woman. Can't stand melodrama. I wondered if you would be available next Wednesday evening. I'm wining and dining our biggest client, Jack Monahugh. It's more social than business, but it would be a great opportunity for you to meet him. Is Ceri available to come along too? What do you think?"

"It's a great idea but I know Ceri already has a meeting booked. It will just be me, is that a problem?"

"No. Not at all. Does Ceri work evenings? She's in advertising too, isn't she? I recognised the name."

"She starts a new job next week but she's also involved in a separate project and it means she's going part-time. She attends a few evening meetings now and again."

I'm tempted to cross my fingers under the table and hold my breath, really hoping Niall doesn't ask what exactly she does outside of her day job. He's a feet on the ground sort of guy and I'm not sure he would understand. Heck, I'm not even sure what

I would say. I need to think about it before I open up that line of conversation. He seems fine, though, and we briefly discuss what sort of background information the client would be interested in hearing. I like Niall, he's a straight talking guy and there are no pretences or half-truths. He does business the old-fashioned way, what you see is what you get, and that is value for money.

As I close the door behind me I sag a little. Nervous energy is eating me up and at this rate I'll run out of steam before the working day has finished. Ceri is attending a group meeting with Mark on Wednesday and I can't expect her to change her plans. Anyway, I'm thinking it will be much better not to involve her any more than necessary, certainly until I know whether Alicia is going to say anything to Niall.

I groan inwardly. Is this bad karma coming back to me because I did something so unforgiveable it doesn't even bear thinking about? Or maybe Ethan was right all along. What if I'm going to start paying the price for ignoring my dreams and making a life with Ceri? Or worse, Ceri is the one who is going to suffer. But why am I in love with her to my very core if it's not meant to be? Who would do that to someone, give them an all-consuming love and then snatch it away? I believe there is a God and I like to think he's compassionate, but I can't see any compassion in wrenching Ceri and me apart. If she knew what I'd done… a part of me deep inside crumples at the thought.

I realise I've been leaning against the wall staring into space for a few minutes and I make my way to the kitchen area for another strong hit of caffeine. My head is full of Ceri: her beautiful smile, those intriguing grey-blue eyes that melt my heart. I love the way her straight blonde hair flicks across her face when she laughs and she inclines her head a little, looking up from under her lashes. The times when she says little and I am left to fill in the gaps, knowing there's no point in talking. Maybe words just can't explain it sometimes. In sombre mood she is a little scary at times but, given the burden she's carrying, that's only to be expected. How does someone live with that? I can understand why she's cautious with people, because the topic often invokes such a strong reaction from people. Non-believers decry it with such vehemence that it can feel like a personal attack. Believers want to know more. Either way it's awkward.

My mindset was that I believe in a God because we can't simply just "be", or have evolved from a state of nothingness. Someone created us and whomsoever it was had a far greater intelligence than any scientist known to man. I also struggle to accept that we end when we die, that the bit that makes each of us unique simply disappears. I literally grilled Ethan when I met up with him, wanting to know the answers to all my questions. Of course it wasn't as simple as that and yes, I have moved on and can now see why so many people believe in life after death.

But the angel thing was a shock. I thought angels belonged to that place we refer to as heaven, which is probably somewhere out there in the universe, where all our energy gathers once we're done here. The existence of multiple lives on earth sounds a bit too sci-fi for me.

Then there is Ceri, and Ethan was adamant his spirit guide told him Ceri is an angel.

Someone bumps my arm and my coffee mug splatters over the worktop.

"Sorry Alex." It's one of the copy editors.

"No problem, I was deep in thought." I nod and make my way back to my desk.

The death of that innocent baby is a black stain on my soul, I'm sure. The fact that Ceri can't sense it means our love obscures her vision. I don't know whether to be grateful about that, or rather sad. How can I tell her something that is bound to alienate her from me?

The truth is that I love her enough to lie, and that's selfish. Totally selfish.

61

Chapter Thirteen – The Week From Hell

I'm beginning to wish that the moment I opened my eyes on Monday morning, I'd rolled back over and refused to play ball. I should have buried myself beneath the covers and disappeared for a week. Everywhere I turn there's a problem. One of the team at work is having a major meltdown over a computer problem that IT can't seem to resolve. Tempers have been frayed to say the least.

Ceri has been very subdued the last couple of days. On Tuesday evening we took a run over to visit my parents, as I knew it was about time I made the introduction. They were fine, but Ceri was very on edge. My parents are the kind of people who hug everyone and want to welcome them into their home whether they know them or not. I could see Ceri wanting to back away and I wondered if it was too much for her. I'm not sure whether she's withdrawn slightly because it obviously marks a turning point for us, or whether she's picked up something negative from me, regarding Alicia.

I'm having real trouble not blurting it all out. It sits on my chest like a heavy weight and I don't think I can carry on much longer knowing I'm deceiving her. I understand her stressing about not letting Mark down, but I have no idea if there is anything else troubling her. Despite everything Ceri has seen and been involved with, she continues to worry about getting it wrong. The idea of picking something up and misinterpreting it, potentially sending someone off in the wrong direction, terrifies her. I find myself doing the counsellor bit, which is a laugh. I told her that if our fate is predetermined, logic would dictate that we can't possibly stray too far from the plan. Her answer stunned me.

"You have been given free will, Alex. Willpower can be a useful tool, but it can also be misused. Whether the intent is good or bad, doesn't really matter. The effect is the same."

She wouldn't say any more. I almost had to sit down, I was so shocked. For a start she said 'you', as in humans, and not 'us'. Should I worry about that? Angels who come here live the same sort of life-span, don't they? She isn't going to suddenly disappear? And secondly, if she was referring to our situation, does that mean she's regretting it and there really is a reason we shouldn't be together? Has Ceri been shown something that proves we've made a big mistake? I try very hard not to ask awkward questions, but I had to know more. She became a little upset and I backed off, fearful of adding to her burden.

Then on Wednesday evening, I hadn't appreciated that the client was going to bring his wife along. Worse still, Niall appeared accompanied by Alicia. Not only was I a spare wheel, I was the centre of the conversation and all eyes were on me. Alicia kept looking away and I was fearful Niall would notice something was up.

At one point I couldn't take anymore. I'd chatted myself hoarse telling them about my career prior to Grey's and avoiding any reference to girlfriends or partners. After a long chat about formula one, which I felt was at least safer ground, I excused myself and headed for the cloakroom. I needed a break, to grab a few quiet moments to compose myself. What I hadn't banked on was Alicia excusing herself shortly after I left the table to waylay me in the lobby.

"I think we need to talk." She handed me a folded piece of paper and her look was one of gentle concern. As our eyes met a pained look passed between us. I nodded, pocketed the slip of paper and made my way back to the table. No one seemed to notice anything odd, but I was glad when the evening was finally over and the goodbyes had been said.

***

"You look totally exhausted," were Ceri's first words as she came through the door and saw me sprawled out on the sofa. "Have you been in long?"

"Ten minutes. A working dinner isn't much fun, I hope your evening was better." I start yanking off my tie and unbuttoning my shirt. I feel strangely closed in, my guilt hugging my chest like a ball and chain.

I watch as she skips around the room, putting her notepad and bag on the table neatly, slipping off her shoes. She's dressed casually tonight: a cherry red top and a great pair of jeans that make her small frame look taller than her five foot three stature. She turns and her hair flies around her face before settling down. One strand is caught by her lipstick and she swishes it away with her hand.

"It went much better than I thought it would. Mark was pleased to say the least!"

She's buzzing with excitement and there's a light in her eyes that seems to illuminate the whole area around her. How could anyone fail to see that Ceri is a very special person? She's an old soul in a young body. I'd heard that said a few times in the past and never really understood what it meant, but I do now. She has such depth of knowledge about some things and yet in other practical areas she often flounders. Her level of understanding is one thing; her ability to cope with life is another. She's strong when she feels she's on safe ground, in a work situation for example. Then with the psychic stuff she seems to have all the answers, but struggles when it comes to dealing with other people's expectations and concerns.

She walks over to the sofa and lowers herself down, snuggling into me. I bury my face in her hair and breathe in the smell of her. Her perfume tonight is citrusy and there's a hint of bergamot which makes it musky. I can't help groaning as my body instantly reacts, wanting her. I know what Ceri needs at this precise moment is to tell me about her evening.

"Did you go solo?" My voice is even, but my heart is doing somersaults. I can't say what other parts of me are doing. Thinking about it will make it worse.

"Yes. After the meditation we sat around in a circle and there was a great deal of positivity flowing. I received two messages, both for people within the group. It wasn't that they were very clear and specific messages, but that I was shown validation that was meaningful to both of the recipients. Mark took me to one side afterwards and said he was astounded. He had no idea I would progress so quickly. He joked with me and said he must be a really awesome teacher!"

She's wriggling around in my arms and with the perfume and the contact this is too much for a guy to take. I disentangle myself and go into the kitchen to pour myself a drink. I'm still having problems trying not to over-think the 'having sex with an angel' thing. A part of me also doesn't want Ceri probing about tonight. I left the hand-written note Alicia handed to me in the car. It simply had a date, time and venue on it. It won't be a problem but I'm torn. I know I need to talk to Alicia, after all these years it's the least I can do. Lying to Ceri is another thing altogether.

I wish there was someone I could talk to as the guilt and remorse is over-shadowing everything I do at the moment. I can only hope that when I eventually find the courage to tell Ceri, she will be able to forgive me.

Chapter Fourteen – Facing The Past

The coffee shop Alicia named in her note was on the other side of town, well away from the office. I arrive half an hour early, which is a big mistake. I've been sitting here nervously fiddling with the menu, my eyes glued to the entrance, ever since I sat down. As she walks through the door she gives me a small smile of recognition and makes her way to the table.

She reaches out to shake hands and it all feels rather awkward.

"Thank you for agreeing to see me Alex. I thought it was best we meet face to face."

I pull out a chair for her and she sits, making no attempt to take off her coat.

"Would you like tea, or perhaps a coffee?"

"Tea would be fine, thank you."

I walk up to the counter to order our drinks and as I walk back to the table she looks away. Her eyes scan around the room and I think she's checking there's no one here who would recognise her.

I sit down and we eye each other nervously, neither knowing who should speak first. I decide it might as well be me.

"Niall doesn't know we… umm… know each other?"

"No, no he doesn't, and it would kill him if he knew. He isn't a jealous man and what is in the past, is in the past. We have tried for many years to have a child and it is his biggest disappointment.

The problem lies with Niall and he feels he's robbed me of the chance to be a mother. If he found out…" She's shaking with the effort of holding herself together.

"Alicia, is there anything I can do? We were both guilty and young people make mistakes. I know that's no excuse—"

"I made the decision that seemed right at the time. What did we know about life, about anything?" The bitterness in her voice is tangible. She stops speaking as the waiter approaches the table, then continues after he's out of earshot. "I listened to the advice I was given and I was afraid of what my parents would say if they found out. My biggest regret is not talking to you about it before that decision was made. Would you really have tried to talk me out of it, if I'd given you a proper chance and listened to what you had to say?"

I sit back for a moment, taking myself back in time. I don't want to give Alicia some glib answer as if I'm emotionally detached from all of this.

"The truth is Alicia, I know I said we could work it out, but I'm not sure I was mature enough at the time to cope with it all. Saying the words to reassure you was one thing, but providing for you and a baby? I was a kid with big ideas, but no life experience and no money. You can't blame yourself. We made this mess, you and I, but it wasn't intentional. We never set out to hurt anyone."

A haunted look appears in her eyes, a look that is so sad I can feel her pain.

"Will we ever be forgiven?" she whispers, her eyes searching mine.

"I don't know Alicia. I like to think that God really is forgiving and understands that if we had been even a couple of years older, it would have been a very different situation."

She looks around, checking no one is within earshot.

"Niall must never find out. It's hard enough that I've had to live with my decision all these years. Maybe I still deserve to suffer, but Niall is a kind and loving man. He would stand by me, but he would be torn into a million different pieces. I won't inflict this on him. You must understand that, Alex, and please promise me you will be careful. You can't tell Ceri, or anyone."

The look on her face is insistent and I feel a lump in my throat for the pain and damage that resulted from our carelessness.

"I'm so sorry, Alicia. This isn't something I've ever discussed with anyone. It's never left me though, not in here." The moment my hand comes to rest against my chest, her tears brim over.

"It's the same for me," her voice is so faint I can hardly hear the words. Her body language reflects the abject hopelessness she's feeling.

"Look, if there's anything I can do, any time at all. If you want to talk or—"

"I've spent my life talking to counsellors and even a psychiatrist. Some old wounds never heal and maybe this one isn't supposed to. Nothing good comes from something bad and I will never forgive myself."

She takes a tissue from her bag, dabs at her eyes, and pushes back on her chair.

"I have to go. But please, this is our secret and it must remain that way. I need you to do this for me."

I nod, unable to speak. She gives me her hand and I put both of mine around hers. I want to hug her, but I feel it would be inappropriate. Her words still ring in my ears as I watch her walk out of the coffee shop.

If I could change one thing in the whole of my life, it would be this, regardless of where that might have taken us in the future.

CERI

Chapter Fifteen – Feeling At Home

For the first time in my earthly life I feel a sense of peace, accept-
ance, and calm. I used to hate the fact that I never felt at ease, always
the one on the outside looking in. Even when I was around people
who were spiritually aware, I knew that my own path was very
different. I just didn't know why. Many ordinary people proclaim
an interest too, but when you start a real discussion you can see
their perception of you change. Often it's because their minds are
closed and what they are really hoping is that they can walk away
thinking you are strange or deluded. Why ask questions if you
aren't prepared to listen and evaluate the response? That puzzled
me for a while, then I realised that people who shun any sort of
belief – whether it's the existence of life after death, religion, or
our in-born sense of belonging to something bigger – need reassurance. Unable to commit, they push everything away, but there
is always that nagging doubt at the back of their minds. What if
hell exists and it really is the place where non-believers end up?
Well, hell on earth surely exists, although it's self-inflicted.

What has brought about the biggest change in me is being with
Alex. Falling in love with someone is one thing, but when they love
you back equally as fiercely it becomes something very different.
I feel confident and it's nothing to do with my enlightenment.
I'm valued, treasured and needed; that invokes a whole host of

emotions I have never experienced before. I make him whole and knowing that makes me feel special.

We seem to be on the same level in virtually everything we do and the goodness in Alex's heart is very healing. He cares about the small things in life and he's sensitive to others in a way that is often missed, but I notice it. He tries to protect me without making it obvious and I love him even more with each passing day. The sun has never shined as brightly, the rain has never been so beautifully refreshing. It's all because of him. I have no idea how long we have together, but I treasure every single second.

Alex has accepted my friendship with Mark, who has been an amazing support and influence. The first time I sat in the group circle and Mark asked if I had any messages, I almost froze. All eyes were on me and suddenly it all became very real. Almost as soon as we had begun meditating a spirit had joined me and they were insistent. The message was for one of the group, Pete, and that concerned me as he had been very quiet all evening. I wished Mark had talked to me about the members beforehand, so I could gauge whether I needed to hold anything back. Messages can be pretty blunt and sometimes words come, but often it's more visual. The message for Pete had been very clear and it was from an older man.

"The gentleman who joined me had a walking stick, but he was swinging it jauntily, rather than using it for support. He found that amusing. We sat for a while on a bench overlooking a large grassy hill. He wore an old jacket with patched elbows and a smart silk handkerchief tucked into the breast pocket. I feel this message is for Pete."

All eyes in the group turned to look at Pete, who shifted in his chair.

"That's okay." He nodded in my direction, indicating that he was happy for me to continue.

"I think he might have worked with cars. I saw detailed drawings and what seemed to be test cars speeding around a track. Not

72

racing cars, but saloon cars. They were all brand new but very old models, which would have made him in his late eighties probably. There was no name, but I know beyond a shadow of a doubt the message is for you. The only words I could hear were 'none of it matters now, so don't dwell on it my son', and he was insistent. The words kept repeating over and over in my head."

I looked up at Pete and he nodded curtly.

"Was there anything else?" Pete narrowed his eyes and I wondered whether he could read my mind.

"I'm not sure... there were some images from his life as we sat together on the bench. Most were to do with cars. There was one thing that was odd: a broken glass crystal rose bowl. I saw someone picking up the pieces, then cleaning up the flowers and water strewn over the floor."

Pete covered his face with his hands, running the heel of his palms back across his eyes. He sniffed and cleared his throat.

"It was my mother's treasured glass bowl. My father bought it for her on their fortieth wedding anniversary. I knocked it over when we were arguing, about a year after her death. He always had flowers in the house because he said it made him feel she was still around. I think it was the smell he identified with. We argued quite a bit and towards the end of his life I had to make some tough decisions. He refused to go into a nursing home, despite the fact that he wasn't really safe living on his own. He was also very sick and in a lot of pain. Often he refused to allow the doctor or nurses in to help. It's always weighed heavily upon me whether or not I did the right thing. Shortly after he died I bought a replacement rose bowl. I never put flowers in it, but it sits on the shelf and I think of them both every time I see it."

"I understand now that he was offering validation by mentioning something very special. He was concerned for you, that was very clear. But I think he was also trying to let you know that he is around you. He is at peace with everything that happened and he recognised your gesture as a way of reaching out to him. There is no need to feel guilty, he's happy and he wants you to enjoy the rest of your life. The emotion he left me with was filled with gratefulness and love. It was touching because it was so strong."

The group sat in silence for a couple of minutes, then Mark asked me if there were any other messages.

"A special visitor," I mused, and everyone looked up at me. "He's a fairly big chappie, a golden retriever. This was someone who loved frolicking in the water, no matter what time of the year it was, and he would have been a very active dog. He kept running around me in a large circle. Can anyone connect with this?"

"Yes," the woman opposite was beaming and looking around the group. "It's Rufus. He was twelve when he died last year and we'd had him since he was ten weeks old. We miss the little devil so much, but we can't bring ourselves to get another pup. That's wonderful Ceri, thank you so much! I can't wait to go home and tell my husband, he'll be thrilled. We keep getting the scent of wet dog and we did wonder… nice to know he's still thinking of us too." She looked thrilled and shrugged her shoulders, as if giving herself a squeeze. "So glad I came tonight!" she added.

After the meeting ended, Pete came up to me and shook my hand.

"Thanks." He looked hesitant. "For what you said, and also what you decided not to share." Our eyes exchanged one meaningful look. What I hadn't mentioned was the fact that his father died of an overdose of medication. It was clear that Pete had been given an ultimatum: *help me to end it all, or get out of my house.* The assumption was made that Pete's father had been confused about the number of tablets he was supposed to take.

Mark said once that most people who sit in circle have a personal reason for wanting to know more. Sometimes it was due to an experience that was so traumatic it affected their energy, and their health. The further they progressed along their spiritual path, the greater the benefits as they learned to shed the burden they carried.

It wasn't the easiest of sessions and I would have preferred my

74

first time solo to have been less intense. I did enjoy meeting Rufus and, as light-hearted as his message had been, it made someone very happy that night.

Chapter Sixteen – A Little Surprise...

Our first three months of living as a couple flew by and we celebrated the evening in style. Well, not quite – we had champagne and a takeaway. Even the champagne was an afterthought and something left over from a party last year. We were both really exhausted though. Alex has his hands full at work and I'm trying to juggle my new job, plus a steep learning curve being tutored by Mark. I accompany him on his weekly visits to a large number of psychic events. Some are informal and often I'm invited to stand up and do a small segment. Other times it's more formal, so I watch and learn. While we really wanted to celebrate, we admitted to each other that we were too tired and the promise of an early night to sleep seemed too good to waste. Alex yawned, then promised he would make it up to me.

A week later he came home from work buzzing.

"What?" I asked, as he bounced into the bedroom. His eyes were sparkling.

"I have a surprise." He waved a small envelope in front of me.

My hands were covered in moisturising cream after a relaxing bath and a facial, so he leant forward and kissed the top of my head.

"Are you going to tell me what it is, or will you make me wait until I've rubbed this in?"

He ripped open the envelope and pulled out a piece of paper, then proceeded to hold it up in front of me so I could read it.

"Alex, that sounds amazing! Why? What have I done to deserve three days in a beautiful French manor house? You do know it isn't my birthday for another two months…"

I stand up and fling my arms around his neck, holding my hands out to avoid covering him with cream. I give him a succession of short, sharp kisses. I can't wipe the smile off my face long enough to give him one long passionate one.

"You deserve it, heck, we both do. I know you booked some time off to spend with Sheena next month, but do you think she'll mind if I whisk you away for three days? I know how much you enjoyed your French trip, despite the circumstances. Niall recommended this place for a romantic getaway. I feel like spoiling you, and having three whole days together will do us both good."

"Of course she won't mind! You won't believe this, but I've been looking online at weekends away and thought I might surprise you. This is awesome. Thank you, thank you, thank you!"

He wraps me tightly in his arms and lifts me off the ground. Alex buries his head in my hair. "I love you, my angel, and I can't wait to take you away."

The coincidence was yet another sign of how we seem to be on the same wavelength.

I know Alex has noticed that I haven't been quite my usual self. My work on the ethereal plane is hard at times and I wish I could keep everything totally separate. It's like having the radio on all the time in the background. If the music is gentle, then it's relaxing. If it's a pounding beat, it's distracting. Often I tune it out. The things I'm doing involve me flitting in and out of people's lives to help them.

With smaller problems, if their spiritual consciousness isn't awakened, they are often totally unaware that I'm with them. It's a case of subtle suggestion on a telepathic level. I send a thought vibration and that's the way I prefer to communicate, because it's easy. As soon as it comes into their minds they act on it and

77

move on with their problem. On earth it's often referred to an inspiration and that amuses me. Do they never stop to consider that one moment their mind is unable to solve a problem and the next the answer is there? Often it's something that would never have occurred to them because they don't have the relevant knowledge or skills.

Then there are the other cases, those suffering a deep trauma that threatens to engulf them and drag them down to a dark place. Individuals with strong beliefs tend to fare better, used to reasoning both sides of a situation and tending towards a positive nature. Others are less grounded, having no sense of security to fall back on when times are tough. Suddenly it all becomes too much. It's referred to as depression and it's a state that only exists here on this plane. Dealing with those cases is much more intense and often the darkness surrounding them means they block out everything. It requires a lot more effort to help and sometimes that means influencing other people's actions to intervene. The problem then becomes complex, like trying to escape from a maze. One wrong turn and any progress made can be undone. I have a woman who has lost her husband after only five years of marriage and she's distraught. She can't see any reason to go on and the earthly part of me keeps getting drawn in as I think of Seb's situation. There is some movement, but each time I succeed in lifting her mood, it's so easy for her to fall back. A part of the problem is that she's taking some tablets prescribed by her doctor. It helps her to relax and sleep, but it isn't easy for me to deal with someone who can't concentrate. I have to work with her via her dreams and that's always difficult.

So many people don't heed the messages we discreetly weave into their dreams. I think, in all honesty, there is a design flaw. Sleep has many levels and on the highest one we interface seamlessly with our true energy on the ethereal plane. But on waking, the person has a whole range of mixed memories and, of course, leaving the body is not a memory that's supposed to remain. So things become garbled. Those who meditate will have a clearer picture than those who don't, simply because it gives them the ability to find that inner place more easily.

The lady I'm working with can only see a future stretching out ahead of her without the person she loves. Somehow I have to get her through this. I know she will survive, as it isn't her time to be called back, but that doesn't make the process any easier. Again, I can't help thinking of Seb and the way that he's being pulled into things that only serve to complicate his life. It's a time when it should be all about healing. Quite simply, it is hell on earth. In both cases, if they could just stand back and let go of their grief for one moment, they would have clarity. It would allow them to circumvent so much of the pain. Neither one of them is at a stage in their spiritual development to appreciate that, so it's purely wishful thinking on my part.

The things that I can't talk to Alex about don't usually cause me a problem. I will admit that when I'm feeling particularly drained emotionally it does affect this side of my life. Sometimes my thoughts are constantly elsewhere, even if that is only for very brief moments at a time.

"I can't wait for this break, Alex, and I promise I will try to totally switch off and concentrate on us."

"That's my girl." He brushes the hair away from my face and looks down at me intently.

"You work too hard and you do need this time away. I know that."

Looking into his eyes is like seeing into his soul. His concern for me is touching and it's a totally selfless act. It's the true sign of a soul chosen to visit this life to be instrumental in the fate of others. They do good works without being consciously aware of their purpose here, but their true vibration is one of healing and guidance.

"I think the universe is sending us back some of the good karma we've been sending out," I grin back at him. "I'm counting down the days."

***

Sheena's visit is relaxing and fun. I suppose Alex and I are like two excited children with our break coming up, so our evenings are light-hearted as we entertain our friend. After the evening meal we stay up late playing board games and laughing. Alex excuses himself around ten o'clock, as he has to leave for work at seven each morning.

"You two go together so well," Sheena remarks, late one night. "I told you there was a Mr Right out there for you. Alex is pretty special, I hope you appreciate him."

"You did and I do, appreciate him that is, all the time. There's a Mr Right for you too," I add.

Sheena looks at me with a slight frown.

"I'm beginning to think that isn't true."

Her aura is a beautiful clear red, indicating a powerful and energetic energy. However, the traits that are associated with that mean Sheena is also very competitive, sexual, and passionate about many things. Sometimes her work life stands in the way of her personal life. I wonder if now is the right time to point that out, because it needs to be said. Kelly is one of her guardian angels and helping to steer her in the right direction. It's obvious that everything will come in time and that there is nothing to fear. Her fate is such that she won't settle down until a little later in life, but I can't see anything untoward, unless that is being hidden from me.

"Your life revolves around your work at the moment and that makes you happy, right?" I throw in, cautiously.

She leans her head back, taking a few moments to contemplate.

"Yes, I love what I do and the fact that I travel extensively and have different experiences. But I know there will come a time when I will tire of this, Ceri. What then?" A sadness creeps over her.

"Then your life will move on when the time is right." I reach across and touch her hand. The life-force I feel is vibrant and positive.

"Don't worry about the future, there's nothing bad. I would tell you if I could sense something to worry about, and you aren't alone."

Immediately she looks at me and I realise I've said something without thinking.

"I don't have spirits around me, do I?" She looks freaked and I detect a hint of fear.

"I didn't mean that." I try to downplay my words, as if she's misunderstood me. "I'm here for you always."

Sheena looks relieved and our attention returns to the Scrabble board. As I pour her another glass of wine I make a mental note to be more careful. Sheena is the closest person I have, after Alex and Seb. She is like a sister to me, but she knows much less about the other side of me now than Alex does and it isn't something she's meant to be involved with.

Chapter Seventeen – Time To Kickback

As Sheena flies off to her next job, Alex and I are busy getting ready for our own trip. She was slightly emotional when we parted, hugging me and making me promise I will ring her when we are safely back home.

There's a slight chill in the air as Alex and I quietly pack the car and it feels as if we are the only ones up and about. At five o'clock in the morning it's a very different world. There's something slightly decadent about being so wide awake and excited. There is little traffic on the road as we begin our journey to the channel tunnel. The miles speed by before the early morning rush hour begins to slow our progress.

We chat, listen to music, and once we are safely aboard the shuttle, we both fall asleep. It's only just over half an hour, but the gentle sway of the carriages speeding along on the rails is blissfully relaxing. Only the announcement over the loudspeaker that we are about to arrive in France stirs us, and our holiday is about to begin.

The manor house, Le Jardin dans le Parc, is truly wonderful. Standing at the entrance to the sweeping drive leading up to the house, it's amazing. The view of the eighteenth century building, set within the beautiful grounds, feels like a glimpse of heaven on earth. With its grand windows and detailed stonework, even on a grey afternoon it's too beautiful for words. Most of the extensive grounds are covered in forest. Only the areas immediately surrounding the house have been cultivated. Rolling lawns, perfectly manicured flower beds and the most stunning display of topiary inspire this image of classic French style. It is indeed a garden within a park and beyond the trees there is a lake that runs close to the rear elevation of the house. Our room is at the front and overlooks the beautiful lawns and rose beds. Walking around to the terraced area, there is a sheer drop down to the edge of the lake. The stone flagstones are covered with a display of potted geraniums. All are still in bloom, although the leaves are beginning to fall as the chilly morning and night air reminds them winter is coming. The pinks, reds, and whites are a mass of blazing colour.

We settle in and realise that communication is going to be a problem. The couple who run the hotel are both Dutch and do not speak any English. Our French isn't the best, so there is a lot of nodding of heads when we go down for dinner.

It's too chilly to eat out on the terrace, but the dining room is very elegant. A cut-glass chandelier graces the centre of the room and doesn't look at all out of place. The floor is varnished and with age is now a dark walnut colour. It creaks as we walk across it, in the comforting way that old floors do. Somehow it makes it feel more like being in someone's home than being in a hotel.

The décor itself is more modern. The circular tables have pale green linen tablecloths and the chairs have cream brocade covers, tied with matching green bows. The attention to detail is both romantic and pleasing to the eye. Each place setting has an array of sparkling crystal glassware and the table centres comprise a white candle rising up from a ring of fresh flowers. It's enchanting as the flickering candlelight reflects off the chandelier and the crystalware, sending little prisms of multi-coloured light everywhere.

Alex pulls out a chair for me, before seating himself.

"Well?" he whispers, leaning forward across the table.

"Perfect! It's wonderful and I love it here."

And perfect it was. The evening was a succession of wonderful food and some amazing wines neither of us had tried before. Everything was served with a genuine respect for the dining experience and great attention to detail. Each of the five small courses was accompanied by a different wine. The glasses were huge and only an inch or two of wine was enough to savour and not obliterate the wonderful flavours of the delicate cuisine. The menu was in French and Dutch, so we decided not to worry too much about the translation and to let each course come as a surprise. It ended with the most delicious tarte tatin – the pastry base caramelised to perfection and layered with apples so thinly sliced they were almost transparent.

The meal wasn't heavy, but we decided to grab our coats and walk around the gardens simply to stretch our legs. Neither of us wanted the evening to end, it was as perfect as a scene from a film. Alex was looking so handsome in his dinner jacket and I felt at ease wearing a long evening dress. As we walked we held hands and then Alex pulled my arm into his.

"You look amazing tonight," his voice sounded heavy with emotion. "Not that you don't look great all the time, but you know what I mean," he added.

"Thank you, I feel good and I think we both brush up rather well!" We laughed. The wine was pleasantly softening our mood, without overwhelming our senses.

"I think I can safely say that this has been the most memorable evening of my life. It's all down to you, my lovely angel. Thank you for agreeing to come away with me."

I burst out laughing.

"It's a hard task but someone had to do it."

He playfully tugged at my arm, safely tucked into his.

"Is it time to head back? There's an incredibly comfortable bed awaiting us and a Jacuzzi for two…"

"Mmm, I think it's that time. Wouldn't it be lovely if life was always like this?" I looked up at the starry sky. From that vantage point, in the middle of extensive grounds and with only a little light pollution from the house spilling out into the darkness, there were millions of little twinkling lights. I wondered how anyone could ever believe there was only the here and now.

"Come on." Alex encouraged me to begin walking back to the house. He pulled my arm a little closer into his body. "I can't wait to find out what you are wearing beneath that gorgeous dress."

"Alex," I admonished, "there you go again."

"I can't help being in touch with my female side." He laughed. "You do look gorgeous and I'm not apologising for using that word. I also can't wait to get my hands on what's underneath and show you what it does to me."

"Okay," I replied meekly. "Sounds good to me."

Chapter Eighteen – A Moment In Time

Sunshine peeks through a gap in the blind and I open my eyes suddenly, remembering we aren't at home. I close them again, snuggling up a little closer to Alex and savouring the peace and quiet. Not a single car or honking of a horn to be heard; only the birds and nothing else.

Alex rolls into me, his eyes still closed. "Wondered when you were going to wake up. This is bliss, isn't it?"

"Mmm, what time is it?"

He props himself up on one elbow to glance at the clock. "Just before seven. Our breakfast in bed will be here soon. We ought to have a bit of a tidy…"

A brief knock on the door and it swings open. I pull the covers up to my chin, but Alex lays there, naked to the waist looking sleepy but cool.

"Bonjour." The patron calmly waltzes in, placing a large tray on the writing desk with hardly a glance. As the door closes we both dissolve into a fit of giggles. I hastily look around the room. I'm sure there isn't anything he hasn't seen before, but the trail of clothes leading to the bathroom is a bit of a giveaway about our evening pursuits.

"I can't believe we left the room in this much of a state." I sit up and survey the rumpled clothes.

"Hey," Alex says over his shoulder, as I adjust my seating position and he hops out of bed to collect the tray. "We had other things occupying our thoughts at the time. A little chaos doesn't hurt once in a while."

However, on his traipse back he places the tray at our feet, then stoops to gather everything up in his arms and deposits the pile on top of an armchair.

"Is that better, Madame?" he enquires.

"Yes, now come and eat breakfast. You said we need to be on the road by eight o'clock and I need a hot shower."

Alex had planned a visit to Versailles and I was thrilled when he suggested it. It's a place I've always longed to visit and even suggested it when I spent time in France with Sheena. I couldn't convince her as she isn't into history, or old buildings. Le Jardin is just north of Paris, so it's an easy journey if we avoid the city and the suburbs, taking the longer route. It's pleasant driving with long stretches of road interspersed with roundabouts and a few small towns.

We expected Versailles to be grand and to have the proportions of a palace, but the size, grandeur and opulence is overpowering. At a time when many people lived in hovels, this was another world entirely. We decide to wander around the grounds before taking the tour inside of the Palace. The sheer scale is bewildering and I'm so excited, wanting to soak up the ambience. You can feel the intrigue and the place is alive with a sense of the generations who have lived, loved and suffered here. Alex purchases a guide book in English and I read out aloud to him as we walk.

"Versailles was regarded as the ultimate example of a royal residence for over a century. It began with Louis XIV and continued to the time of Louis XVI. Versailles is a wealthy suburb of Paris now, but originally it was merely a country village. It became the centre of political power from the late 1600s. How's your history?" I take a peek at his glazed look.

"Not too good."

I skim the pages and then flick through. In the middle there's a map of the grounds.

"Okay, we'll head in this direction. You've heard of the Petit Trianon, Louis XVI gave it as a gift to his wife, Marie Antoinette? She was only nineteen at the time. The small château was meant to keep her occupied and she whiled away her time redesigning the garden in the latest English fashion. The Petit Trianon was originally built for Louis XV's mistress, Madame de Pompadour, but it became famous for being associated with Marie Antoinette's extravagances. Only the Queen's inner circle were invited as it was reputed to be a place of intimacy and pleasure, away from the prying eyes of court life. Imagine someone so young having all that responsibility, she was only fifteen years of age when she was married. Alex, thank you for bringing me here, I absolutely love it!"

"I can tell," he replies, smirking. We stop at the top of several flights of sweeping stone steps to survey the Grand Canal, which the guide book tells us is an incredible sixty two metres wide and fifteen hundred metres long. It seems to stretch endlessly into the distance and even Alex is speechless. He stands at my side, taking in a scene that simply cannot be described. Grand or magnificent seem to hardly do it justice.

We wander along the gently curving path that takes us away from the astounding view and find ourselves surrounded by manicured lawns, vast flower beds, sculptures, and ornate fountains. Everywhere there are little hidden corners and my mind conjures up pictures of clandestine meetings between lovers.

"You love this stuff, don't you?"

I laugh. "It shows, does it?"

We've been following a tall hedge and it opens up to a little vantage point, a simple terrace surrounded by a stone wall and with a wide stone bench.

"Sit," Alex commands and at first I laugh at his tone, then I see his face is serious. I put the guide book down, feeling guilty I've bored him. It's easy for me to submerse myself in the history and my romantic imaginings of life at court. But then, as a teen I was an avid reader of historical romance mainly because, I suppose, it was a form of escapism.

He turns away from me as I sit, to look out across the view. When he turns back to face me he has something in his hand.

"Ceri, I brought you here today for a reason." He walks towards me, kneeling at my side on the dusty ground so that our eyes are level. "I can't imagine ever being without you. The point of bringing you here was because I wanted to show you that, in terms of this life, we are a dot on the timeline of history. This dot, though, is the most important thing in the world to me. I'm not saying to you that what you know about everything out there isn't relevant, but our togetherness has a place too. Will you accept this?"

He takes my hand and turns it palm upwards, then places a ring in the centre of it. It's white gold, with one single diamond in a square setting. It's beautiful. I sit here for a few moments as tears fill my eyes. This little corner is protected from the wind and the hedge stifles any sounds from the grounds immediately surrounding the main buildings. It's as if we are alone here and time stands still. His eyes have not moved from mine, but words are hard to find.

"Alex, are you asking me to marry you?" I whisper, my throat hoarse from holding back a full flood of tears.

"I know we could just go on as we are, but I need 'us' to be official. I want to tell the world I've found my soul mate and I don't intend letting her go. Is that selfish of me?"

"Alex, you don't have a selfish bone in your body. But do you know what you are getting yourself into? We're still feeling our way along and what if something gets in the way? I don't want to think of hurting you ever, and I don't want you to have a false sense of security. I can't see our future. I just hope and pray it's one that sees us being together until this life is over."

He bends his head and I can feel the emotion within him. He throws his arms around me and hugs me so tightly I can scarcely breathe.

"I'm not asking for guarantees, I'm only asking you to accept this symbol of my love for you. It's a promise that when the time is right we'll make it official, God willing."

I nod, wiping away the tears that escape, despite the enormous effort I'm making not to let them flow. Tears of happiness and sadness too, hope for our future together and prayers that this is something our fate will grant us.

"Alex, as long as I am here on this earth I am yours, that's my promise," I whisper into his ear. It's enough and we sit entwined, while the wind playfully messes our hair and the magical backdrop of Versailles casts a spell over us both.

This was meant to be.

Chapter Nineteen – Announcements

Alex's proposal was a total surprise and I didn't see it coming. He admitted to me that he had confided in Sheena about his intentions and asked her opinion. That worried me slightly – what if he'd let anything slip? Obviously that wasn't the case, or Sheena would have said something, but it was yet another sharp reminder that our situation isn't straightforward.

We are both excited to share our news, of course, although we've decided not to set a date or to feel any pressure about arranging a wedding. It also presents me with a headache. Telling my parents is going to be a problem, but more importantly sharing our news with Seb. It's not something I feel able to do by email and when I ring him I'm rather relieved to hear he sounds more like his old self.

"It's lovely to hear your voice, Sis," his words reflect warmth and he's genuinely pleased.

"I wondered how you were doing. And I have some news."

"I'm fine. You have to stop worrying about me, I'm surviving. Quite frankly, with some of the things I've seen since I've been travelling, it serves to remind me that I still have a lot for which I need to be grateful. I've moved on again and I've met up with a group doing work for a social enterprise agency. It's unpaid, but there's free accommodation and a small allowance. So what's your news?"

"Alex and I are engaged, we aren't setting a date or anything heavy like that. It's just the next step."

He immediately replies and I can hear he's happy for us. "About time! He's a great guy, Ceri, and I thought that from the start. Wish I knew him a bit better, but such is life. Do I sense some hesitation though? I always thought you'd be the one to tie the knot first and not me."

The irony of that is so sad, but I know what Seb means. I want to be excited and do the bride thing, although I would choose to do that in a low-key way. Seb has no idea that it isn't that simple. I still find it hard to believe that fate is smiling upon us.

"Life is busy at the moment and we both have new jobs. There's so much we should catch up on, you know. Do you see yourself coming home, even for a short visit? I could send the money for the air fare?"

He pauses and I can feel he's torn, but the answer is said without hesitation. "No, I have to discover who I am so I can move forward. I think I'll know when I've found something that feels right. For now I'm happy to try anything that comes along. At least at the moment I feel I'm being useful. Every single day I see hardship that you wouldn't believe. It's a sad world at times."

"I know, but always remember that you can only do so much. Don't take the weight of the world on your shoulders, do your bit and try to live with what you can't change."

"The only way to survive here is to understand you can only help to relieve the suffering for a few. Sometimes even that is a temporary thing. It's better than doing nothing at all."

"I'm proud of you Seb, and I love you."

"Don't run away from the marriage thing, Ceri. Embrace it. You take life too seriously at times and you never know what's around the corner, take it from me. Grab the good things that life has to offer and feel blessed."

It strikes me that my brother is changing in ways I hadn't even considered. From being a man with a totally closed mind, he is gradually learning that life is multifaceted. What you see depends upon where you are standing and what your life experiences have been. He has taken the first step on his own path of enlightenment.

***

"We should have a party," Alex mumbles, his mouth full of potato chips.

"Why?"

"Because it's a bit mean-spirited simply sharing the news. We're doing everyone out of all the free food and drink that usually accompany an engagement party."

I groan.

"Seriously, Ceri, think about it. We can invite your parents and that will be so much easier than travelling down to see them. I know you've been ignoring it, but you can't keep them in the dark forever. Especially now that you've told Seb, it seems unfair. We can still keep it small, but it would be nice to invite a few work friends too. Niall has already asked if we are having a party."

I feel as if my back is up against a wall. When I said "yes" I was only thinking about Alex and myself, forgetting that other people around us will have expectations.

"All right, but we keep it to the minimum." Alex moves in for his trademark hug, picking me up and twirling me around. "Now put me down and go and find a venue. I'll organise the food, but that's it."

"You must be a little bit excited, admit it." He flashes me his stupid grin.

"No, it's all a pain and it means I have to phone my parents sooner rather than later. See what you've started?"

"Ring them after we've eaten, don't let it cast a shadow over things. Remember that everyone else at the party will be there because we want them to be, they'll be happy for us. You never know, your parents might feel the same way too."

When I ring to break the news I'm glad Alex is in the other room. My father answers the phone and without saying anything other than "Hello Ceri," he immediately puts down the handset. There are a few minutes of silence.

"Hello?" Clearly he didn't bother to mention who was calling.

"It's Ceri, Mum."

"Oh, hello Ceri, that's unexpected. Seb doesn't have a problem, does he?" Her voice becomes anxious.

"No, he's fine. I spoke to him yesterday. I'm ringing with some news of my own."

"I do worry about him so and we miss Anna, she was such a lovely young woman. Is he talking about coming back home?"

"No, not at the moment. Give him some time Mum, he isn't ready quite yet. He's discovering who he is and thinking about what he wants to do with the rest of his life."

Her voice turns cold. "Why is he suddenly so unsure of himself? You haven't been advising him, have you? Seb was always the one who knew where he was going. Look at the wonderful experiences he's had and now he's reached the point in his life where he needs to settle down."

"Look Mum, when you find someone to love it never crosses your mind you will lose them. What Seb's going through is quite normal given the tragic circumstances." I wish I hadn't dialled the number. Alex can't understand how every time I talk to my parents it turns into a disaster.

"You are hardly an expert, but Seb going off to discover himself sounds more like you talking, than Seb. He needs to move on and find someone else."

I'm almost speechless with anger. Not least because in one breath she is dismissing Seb's loss as if it's one of those things, suggesting he should now look for a replacement.

"I haven't called to argue. I want to tell you that I'm engaged and Alex and I are throwing a party. I will send you an invitation in the post. If you are both free it would be an opportunity for you to meet him. Work is very busy at the moment and I can't really take off any time to come and visit."

There's a moment's silence.

"Oh, I see. And who exactly is this Alex?"

"The man I've fallen in love with. I'll send that invitation out to you this weekend."

I hit the end call button and sit, my nerves on edge. There seems to be absolutely no connection whatsoever between my parents and myself. I will have to sit Alex down and explain that he can't have any expectations when it comes to meeting them, or he's going to be in for a big disappointment.

Chapter Twenty – When The Past Catches Up

"Time to party." Alex stands over me as I'm leaning in to straighten the flower arrangement on the drinks table.

"Well, the buffet looks great and the room is perfect. Let's hope the guests behave themselves." I grimace. I'm not a party person at the best of times and the thought of introducing my parents to Alex's family makes me want to roll my eyes. It will be fire meets ice. Alex can tell I'm worried and I will be so glad when this night is over.

"Come on," he taunts, flashing me his grin. "Relax. It's supposed to be a celebration. Let me see that ring." He grabs my hand, holding it up for inspection. "Divine. And the ring isn't bad either." He laughs.

"It is beautiful and you look awesome." I lean into him and plant a soft kiss on his neck. "In case I forget to mention it later, I'm very proud to be engaged to you, Alex. I love you more than I could ever have thought possible."

We hug for a few minutes, drawing breath before the guests begin to arrive.

"Any last minute instructions?" he asks nervously.

"Yes. You are doing the intros for the parents and I'm staying well away. Rescue your parents before the conversation deteriorates and that's an order. How about you? Anything I need to be wary of?"

He looks at me as if he's giving it some serious thought. "Hey, I was only joking," I add.

"Consider it done," he says, as he heads off to the reception area. "By the way, did I tell you that I am the luckiest man alive?"

"Many times, now go!"

I pop up to the room The Bell Inn have set aside for us to change in. My dress is laid out on the bed and I take my time getting ready. I figure it's a little bit like practising to be the bride, everyone will be expecting me to arrive fashionably late. There's a knock on the door and I hear Sheena's voice.

"Come in!"

"Hey, how are you doing girl?" She waltzes in looking very glamorous and with shining eyes. "I've brought a plus one as instructed and he just might be someone special!"

Her excitement is infectious. It seems the party has begun.

***

Sheena does my hair, piling it high on top of my head with one single tendril curling down around each side of my face. It's a new me and it looks good. She helps me to slip on the floor length gown, and standing back to look at myself I feel elegant. The colour on the label said nude. It's a very soft pink with a strappy top, falling in simple folds from my waist to the floor. A thin silver belt matches the silver necklace and earrings Alex helped me choose.

"You look amazing, Ceri!" Sheena sighs. "You'll be a bride next and that means I'll be a bridesmaid yet again."

"Not for a long time yet, so there's still time for you to beat me to the altar." We burst out laughing.

"Now there's a thought." She chuckles. "Are you ready?"

"As ready as I'm ever going to be. I really need a drink though."

"Follow me, I know a man who might be able to remedy that

little predicament for you."

As we descend the staircase the buzz of music and laughter filters up from the function room. There are already about twenty people inside and we head over to Alex. He's talking to someone I don't know and Sheena immediately introduces him as her plus one.

"This is Sam, we work together." We shake hands and I manage to stop myself from saying that Sheena has kept this very quiet. She hasn't ever mentioned him to me before and I flash an inquisitive look her way. She blushes.

"Great to meet you, Ceri. Congratulations on your engagement. Alex was just telling me that you recently visited the palace at Versailles. I'll have to remember that for the future if I ever decide to get engaged."

I take an instant liking to him.

Behind us the room is filling up and people are searching for us, gifts and cards in hand. Alex steers me away and in the direction of Niall and Alicia, who have just arrived. Niall is carrying a large, beautifully wrapped present.

"Ceri, Alex, congratulations you two! Alicia chose this, I have no idea what it is, but it's heavy." He hands the parcel to Alex to place on the present table, which I notice already has a small mound of boxes and a stack of cards. Niall kisses my cheek and shakes Alex's hand. I lean in to air kiss Alicia and she says a quiet, "Thank you for the invitation. I hope you two will be very happy."

"Our pleasure, and you really shouldn't have," I add, feeling slightly embarrassed.

"I hope you like it, Alex mentioned you love cooking." Before I can reply with a quip that I'm sort of banking on Alex being in the kitchen more than I am, Alex is at my side and whisks me away to meet his work colleagues.

It's one long round of meet and greet. Then I spot my parents arriving. I nudge Alex and he leaves me to chat whilst he takes care of them. Following behind is Mark and his wife, Sarah, so I excuse myself. As Mark introduces us, I look up to see Alex's parents, Tony and Helen, wander in. I grab Sheena and ask her to sort out drinks for Mark and Alicia, then make my way over to Tony and Helen. They both hug me as they would a daughter and I can tell they are thrilled to be here celebrating our engagement.

"Alex is over here, talking to my parents." It's the worst scenario: I was hoping I wouldn't be around for this bit. Alex has already spotted us and heads across the room with my parents in tow and we meet in the middle.

He gives his mum a kiss and a hug, then shakes his father's hand vigorously. His father leans in to put his hand on Alex's shoulder and give a hefty pat. At that precise moment three of the people I work with arrive and I make my apologies, leaving Alex to deal with it. A sigh of relief escapes my lips as I walk away and I only hope no one has heard it.

I sort out drinks for the guys, and walk them across to Sheena's little group to get acquainted. It's a juggling act and I'm exhausted already. I'm about to grab myself a big glass of wine when I see a familiar face appear in the doorway.

"Seb!" I screech and run the length of the room, jumping into his arms. Tears of joy run down my face and I wipe them away with the back of my hand. "How did you get here? You never said…"

"I asked him." Alex is at my side as Seb releases me. I turn and Alex throws his arms around me.

"I knew it would make you happy," he says and leans across to shake hands with Seb. I study my brother's face. He's heavily tanned and he looks well, but much slimmer and tired. Gone is the carefree guy who meandered through life and standing in his place is someone who is a survivor. There is a new sense of strength about him. Maybe determination is a better description. My mind is whirling and then I remember that Alex has left our respective parents alone.

"Come and say hello to Mum and Dad," I say, dragging Seb across the room. As we head in their direction it's obvious they are making polite conversation that is a bit strained. As soon as my parents see Seb they stop talking and there are a few tearful eyes. Everyone is interesting in hearing about the latest project Seb's been involved with and it's a relief. It breaks the ice.

Alex and I slide away to grab two glasses of wine.

"Alex, that was a totally amazing thing to do! Seb told me you sent him a return ticket, you are the best, do you know that?" I reach up on tip toe to kiss his cheek.

"What makes you happy makes me happy too, angel."

Alex's father suddenly appears at my side, carrying two empty glasses to be refilled. He smiles at me and inclines his head to Alex, indicating a group of people standing by the window.

"Alex, I just bumped into Alicia. You didn't mention you were in touch after all these years. What a lovely surprise."

The colour drains from Alex's face and he shoots me a glance. I open my mouth to speak, but I can tell from Alex's reaction that now is not the right time. I help his father top up the glasses and he walks back to the group gathered around Seb.

"Alex?" I don't know quite what to say to him.

"It's a long story and one I should have told you when we first met. I'll explain later, I promise." We kiss briefly. I'm still a little stunned, but pull myself together. Not least because I'm anxious to check on what my parents are talking about and whether the subject of their difficult daughter has yet raised its head.

I leave Alex and walk back to them. The room is buzzing with laughter, soft music and happiness. We're getting through this and another two hours and it will all be over. Seb is home for a while at least and I'm feeling happy. The only worry is that Alex is uncomfortable and I don't know if I should be worried. I purposely walk past Niall and Alicia, who are still talking to Sheena and Sam. I walk straight past, but as I do Alicia suddenly turns, totally unaware I'm behind her. We bump slightly, she apologises and I smile as she heads in the direction of the cloakroom.

Something inside me groans, oh no, not that. I continue walking. That moment of intense pain, guilt, and desperation that hit me when Alicia and I touched remains with me. I look around for Alex and our eyes meet across the room. He stares at me for one lingering moment and absentmindedly runs a hand through his hair in a solitary act of desperation.

No words are necessary. His soul is crying out *forgive me*.

Printed by RR Donnelley at Glasgow, UK